John Dryden, Geoffrey Chaucer

Dryden's Palamon and Arcite

The knight's Tale - Volume 5

John Dryden, Geoffrey Chaucer

Dryden's Palamon and Arcite
The knight's Tale - Volume 5

ISBN/EAN: 9783337100537

Printed in Europe, USA, Canada, Australia, Japan

Cover: Foto ©Andreas Hilbeck / pixelio.de

More available books at **www.hansebooks.com**

The Silver Series of English Classics

DRYDEN'S

PALAMON AND ARCITE

OR, THE KNIGHT'S TALE

EDITED WITH INTRODUCTION AND NOTES

BY

ALEXANDER S. TWOMBLY

SILVER, BURDETT AND COMPANY

NEW YORK   BOSTON   CHICAGO

1898

INTRODUCTION.

It is difficult to reproduce a satisfactory portraiture of the poet Dryden, from the conflicting opinions expressed concerning him in various biographical sketches. It is easy to give the leading events in his life; it is possible to show the peculiarities of his literary talent, and to award him the position of "the father of English criticism, who first taught us to determine, upon principles, the merit of composition." But as to the *man*, the portrait handed down to us by his friends is too flattering; that which his rivals and enemies painted, in satire and epigram, is obviously colored by prejudice.

Judging him by his writings alone, we have a two-sided character; looked upon from one side, we see a flatterer, disguising his sycophancy in the charm of his style; a trimmer in politics and religion; a writer who was willing to degrade his genius to suit the depravity of his times; and a plagiarist who did not scruple to borrow material for his plays and tragedies. From the other standpoint, we discover that Dryden's dedications to his patrons, containing what seems to us fulsome adulation, were, after the manner of his age, common to all writers, whether obliged to live by patronage or not; we find that the poet was apparently as sincere in his "Heroic Stanzas on the late Lord Protector," in 1658, as he was loyal to the "powers that be" in his "Astræa Redux," when Charles II. was restored; and that after King James' accession he was more truly actuated by his zeal for Rome when he wrote his "Hind and Panther," than he was ever actuated by any other religious motive.

If, in the first and longest part of his literary career, he yielded in his writings to the debauched taste of the period and wrote a score of plays which are low and often indecent, he at least, in later years, came to better things, confessed his folly, and (in 1697) wrote his "Alexander's Feast," "a masterpiece of rapture and art"; also "Religio Laici" (1682), almost his only work which was "a voluntary effusion"; and other poems and translations which are an honor to his heart as well as to his talent.

Allowing, in conclusion, that he appropriated the material of earlier writers, he never attempted to defend the practice, nor to deny the charge, but claimed that, by adding so much of his own, English poetry became almost a new art under his hand.

As to his mental ability, no one has doubted that he possessed a "singularly solid and judicious mind"; was an "excellent reasoner," strong in discussion, citing valuable authorities, and in method showing great good sense. Unfortunately his subject-matter was beneath his art as a writer, and too large a portion of his better poems consisted of translations and adaptations.

Personally, he was supremely conscious of his own powers, demanding recognition of his merit, ostentatious, jealous of rivals, and fond of familiarity with great personages; but that he could win and keep a friend, is evident from Congreve's estimate of his humane, compassionate, and forgiving nature, which made him ready to assist other writers in correcting their errors in composition, as well as easy of access to those who were disposed to treat him fairly.

Under all these varying lights and shadows, we have a composite character, which defies exact portraiture. In these later days, such a personage could hardly exist, so changed are the standards and conditions of life. Even a poet must to-day conform, in his conduct and writings, to the better ideals of art and morality.

Let it be remembered, then, that John Dryden was born in 1631; that his father, the son of Sir Erasmus Dryden, baronet of Cannons Ashby, was an Anabaptist, a faith which was repulsive to the poet; that John was one of the King's Scholars at Westminster School, under the famous Dr. Busby, when school life was anything but helpful to good morals, and that he was elected, in 1650, to one of the Westminster Scholarships at Cambridge, but went off to Trinity College and was admitted to a Bachelor's degree in 1653, a period of English history when many nobles possessed nothing of nobility but the name, when the lords could travel only with an armed retinue, and foot-pads invested the highways.

It was a time when the tenements of London were so bad that a plague carried off hundreds of thousands of their inhabitants, and coarse sensuality was so prevalent that the country squire vied in scurrility of language with the lowest clown. A chaplain could be obtained for his board and a small stipend. Sometimes he even curried his employer's horses and was a sort of an upper menial of the household.

In literature, no playwright could live unless he pandered to a mocking, gross constituency, which demanded tragedies with every possible adjunct of "blood and thunder," and comedies which no respectable woman could hear. No wonder that Dryden, in such times and with his easy-going conscience, wrote "The Wild Gallant" in his earlier days, and "The Spanish Friar" as late as 1681.

It was also a period when authors copied the example of statesmen and legislators, and flattered the great and powerful, the recompense being an office or a purse of gold. If a king were the patron, a pension was the reward of still baser sycophancy. The authors revenged themselves by holding a petty court of their own, in some London coffee-house, and received the homage of the lesser lights in literature. At "Will's," Dryden sat in the warmest nook by the fire in winter, and on the balcony in the shade in summer, "a pinch from his snuff-box being honor sufficient to turn the head of a young enthusiast." Pope, when a boy, having been introduced to Dryden, at Will's, boasted of the interview all his life.

As to his genius, there can be no doubt that Dryden was the first literary light of his times. He stood between Milton, who died in 1674, and the so-called Classic Age, in which writers like Addison, Swift and Pope elevated the standard of letters, amid less turbulent surroundings. He made poetry readable, improved the versification, and made a permanent impression as a critic, satirist, and story-teller on the mind of the English nation. His fables were pleasant reading for the people, and, as he says in his " Prologue," he selected such stories of old authors as contained an instructive moral. Dr. Johnson thinks that Dryden " seldom struggled after supreme excellence; that he was willing to enjoy fame on the easiest terms, and that when he could content others, was himself contented." It is said that he never corrected or improved his works after they were published.

In his " Absalom and Achitophel," he inaugurated a series of stinging satires which were unsurpassed in that line, and in " Religio Laici " (The Religion of a Layman), he magnified the Protestant faith. In the " Hind and Panther," he argued for the Romish Creed which he had accepted, and although he was ridiculed because in the fable the two animals talked theology, yet his ability no one could challenge.

At last, having written five dramas and a translation of five of the Satires of Juvenal and the whole of Persius in four or five years, he reached the summit of his literary fame when, in 1694, he wrote his translation of Virgil's " Æneid," which Pope called " the most noble and spirited translation in any language." For this work, the author received £1300.

" The Fables," or stories reproduced and embellished from Chaucer and Boccaccio, were his latest works. These were written in the sad, declining years of his life : Shadwell, an old enemy whom he had stigmatized as Og, had succeeded him as poet-laureate; King James, who had been his patron, was in exile; the poet's religion was despised in England ; his family was a burden, — he had married Lady Elizabeth Howard, and of his three sons he was obliged to support one abroad, — and he was impoverished, having lost all his emoluments.

Forced to ask loans and even to pawn his watch to raise money for his son, he became querulous at Fortune's neglect of him. After having been for some time a cripple in his limbs, he died May 1, 1700, of gangrene in the leg.

Dr. Johnson, in his "Life of Dryden," repeats a story of the poet's extraordinary funeral, which was "tumultuous and confused," because interrupted and delayed by a son of the Lord Chancellor, with some of his rakish companions, who demanded a more public demonstration. This story Dr. Johnson says he "intended to omit, as it appears with no great evidence"; but it at least gives an idea of the rude manners of those times.

We may be sure, in any event, that the poet was honored in his burial; for he was laid in the Poet's Corner, in Westminster Abbey, among the honored dead, the simple word "Dryden" being inscribed on his tablet, to signify that as a great man of letters, Dryden needed no eulogistic inscription to remind the world of his genius, or to perpetuate his fame.

THE POETIC TALE.

The "Canterbury Tales," from which Dryden adapted his story of "Palamon and Arcite," were written by Geoffrey Chaucer, about the middle of the fourteenth century. Chaucer has been called the Father of our English Literature, "compared with whose productions all that precedes is barbarism." Long before his age, the English language had received a strong tincture of the French, although its form remained Saxon. Many of the words and much of the meter could not easily be understood by Englishmen even in Dryden's time; therefore it was a great boon to his countrymen when the poet, in the seventeenth century, modernized the pleasing stories of Chaucer, and introduced them, with all their heroic suggestions of chivalry and their quaint fables, in a readable and delightful style.

The story of "Palamon and Arcite" had been adapted by Chaucer from the "Teseide" of Boccaccio, who had found the plot in the "Thebais" of Statius, a Latin poet. Of his own version Dryden says, in his preface, "I have not tied myself to a literal translation, but have often omitted what I judged unnecessary, or not of dignity enough to appear in the company of better thoughts. I have presumed farther in some places, and added somewhat of my own where I thought my author was deficient and had not given his thoughts their true luster, for want of words in the beginning of our language. And to this I was the more emboldened because I found I had a soul congenial to his, and that I had been conversant in the same studies."

The other fables and tales which Dryden "adapted" from Chaucer are "The Cock and the Fox," "The Flower and the Leaf," "The Wife of Bath's Tale," and (from the "Prologue") "The Character of the Good Parson." Dryden liked the "Palamon and Arcite" the best, and we may well agree with him, as we read in this tale of war and tournament, of courtly knights and high-born ladies, of ancient ceremonies and pageants and all the chivalrous deeds and manners of the ancient times.

The scene is laid principally at Athens, and the actors

are as grand and noble, according to the ideas of antiquity, as the heroes of the "Iliad" and the "Odyssey," with more of the polish and splendor of the classic Athenian age. Romantic love, with its heroic and extravagant sentiments; unexpected situations and their development in large results; the supernatural, with the peculiar actions of the gods and goddesses, and even the weaknesses of the women of the story, with the enigmatical Emily in the foreground, make a picture having all the color and magnificence that one can desire in a tale of the earlier romance.

There are some lengthy passages, as, for example, Arcite's dying "oration" to Emily and Palamon and the speech of Theseus at the marriage ceremony, full of jarring notes, mingled with thanks to "the gracious gods for what they give." These may seem to us far-fetched and rather monotonously absurd; but they are no more peculiar than the conversation between Diomed and Glaucus and other speeches in the "Iliad" of Homer.

There are also some blemishes, such as overwrought exuberance of style and falsity in cadences, which are attributable to the later poet; but, as a whole, the story of "Palamon and Arcite," as told by Dryden, is delightful in its freshness, brilliant in its style, lofty in its tone, and creating a marvelous sense of reality in the scenes and characters of an age so alien to our own.

As to the versification, Dryden's line of ten syllables, with five feet, is the same as that of Chaucer, with the rhymed couplet. Pope may have taken the rhymed couplet from Dryden for his "Iliad." There are, however, many passages with three lines ending in the same rhyme; this is the "triplet" form, which is sometimes used to complete the sense more effectively than by the rhymed couplet. For the same reason, apparently, Dryden sometimes makes use of the line of twelve syllables, with six feet, which is called the Alexandrine meter, a kind of verse borrowed from the French, which Pope characterizes thus:

> "A needless Alexandrine ends the song,
> That like a wounded snake, drags its slow length along."

The alliterations of Dryden in this poem may also be noticed, as they often add vigor to the sense. As to the rhymes used by Dryden, it should be said that they sound, to a modern English ear, better than many of Chaucer's; this, however, may be a matter merely of difference in the pronunciation.

The couplet of Dryden —

> "By fortune he was now to Venus trined,
> And with stern Mars, in Capricorn was joined" —

shows how rhyme may be affected by pronunciation, some English-speaking people, even in our day, pronouncing "joined" as if it rhymed with "trined."

Many words used by Chaucer are now obsolete, and so many have acquired a new meaning that a full glossary is an absolute necessity to the student who would understand and enjoy draughts from "the well of English undefiled" of the old poet. But there is also a number of similar words, which Dryden has introduced to give quaintness to his version. A glossary is therefore given, that the reader may leave no word or sentence of "The Knight's Tale" uncomprehended.

PALAMON AND ARCITE;

OR, THE KNIGHT'S TALE.

———oo⦂⦂oo———

BOOK I.

In days of old there lived, of mighty fame,
A valiant prince, and Theseus was his name;
A chief who more in feats of arms excelled,
The rising nor the setting sun beheld.
Of Athens he was lord; much land he won,   5
And added foreign countries to his crown.
In Scythia with the warrior queen he strove,
Whom first by force he conquered, then by love;
He brought in triumph back the beauteous dame,
With whom her sister, fair Emilia, came.   10
With honour to his home let Theseus ride,
With Love to friend, and Fortune for his guide,
And his victorious army at his side.
I pass their warlike pomp, their proud array,
Their shouts, their songs, their welcome on the way;   15
But, were it not too long, I would recite
The feats of Amazons, the fatal fight
Betwixt the hardy queen and hero knight;
The town besieged, and how much blood it cost
The female army and the Athenian host;   20
The spousals of Hippolyta the queen;
What tilts and turneys at the feast were seen;
The storm at their return, the ladies' fear:
But these and other things I must forbear.

15

The field is spacious I design to sow,   25
With oxen far unfit to draw the plough:
The remnant of my tale is of a length
To tire your patience, and to waste my strength;
And trivial accidents shall be forborne,
That others may have time to take their turn,   30
As was at first enjoined us by mine host,
That he whose tale is best, and pleases most,
Should win his supper at our common cost.
     And therefore where I left, I will pursue
This ancient story, whether false or true,   35
In hope it may be mended with a new.
The prince I mentioned, full of high renown,
In this array drew near the Athenian town;
When, in his pomp and utmost of his pride
Marching, he chanced to cast his eye aside,   40
And saw a quire of mourning dames, who lay
By two and two across the common way:
At his approach they raised a rueful cry,
And beat their breasts, and held their hands on high,
Creeping and crying, till they seized at last   45
His courser's bridle and his feet embraced.
     "Tell me," said Theseus, "what and whence you are,
And why this funeral pageant you prepare?
Is this the welcome of my worthy deeds,
To meet my triumph in ill-omened weeds?   50
Or envy you my praise, and would destroy
With grief my pleasures, and pollute my joy?
Or are you injured, and demand relief?
Name your request, and I will ease your grief."
     The most in years of all the mourning train   55
Began; but sounded first away for pain;
Then, scarce recovered, spoke: "Nor envy we
Thy great renown, nor grudge thy victory;
'Tis thine, O king, the afflicted to redress,

And fame has filled the world with thy success:　60
We wretched women sue for that alone,
Which of thy goodness is refused to none;
Let fall some drops of pity on our grief,
If what we beg be just, and we deserve relief;
For none of us, who now thy grace implore,　65
But held the rank of sovereign queen before;
Till, thanks to giddy Chance, which never bears
That mortal bliss should last for length of years,
She cast us headlong from our high estate,
And here in hope of thy return we wait,　70
And long have waited in the temple nigh,
Built to the gracious goddess Clemency.
But reverence thou the power whose name it bears,
Relieve the oppressed, and wipe the widows' tears.
I, wretched I, have other fortune seen,　75
The wife of Capaneus, and once a queen:
At Thebes he fell; cursed be the fatal day!
And all the rest thou seest in this array
To make their moan, their lords in battle lost,
Before that town besieged by our confederate host.　80
But Creon, old and impious, who commands
The Theban city, and usurps the lands,
Denies the rites of funeral fires to those
Whose breathless bodies yet he calls his foes.
Unburned, unburied, on a heap they lie;　85
Such is their fate, and such his tyranny;
No friend has leave to bear away the dead,
But with their lifeless limbs his hounds are fed."
At this she shrieked aloud; the mournful train
Echoed her grief, and grovelling on the plain,　90
With groans, and hands upheld, to move his mind,
Besought his pity to her helpless kind.
　The prince was touched, his tears began to flow,
And, as his tender heart would break in two,

He sighed; and could not but their fate deplore,   95
So wretched now, so fortunate before.
Then lightly from his lofty steed he flew,
And raising one by one the suppliant crew,
To comfort each, full solemnly he swore,
That, by the faith which knights to knighthood bore,   100
And whate'er else to chivalry belongs,
He would not cease, till he revenged their wrongs;
That Greece should see performed what he declared,
And cruel Creon find his just reward.
He said no more, but shunning all delay   105
Rode on, nor entered Athens on his way;
But left his sister and his queen behind,
And waved his royal banner in the wind,
Where in an argent field the God of War
Was drawn triumphant on his iron car;   110
Red was his sword, and shield, and whole attire,
And all the godhead seemed to glow with fire;
Even the ground glittered where the standard flew,
And the green grass was dyed to sanguine hue.
High on his pointed lance his pennon bore   115
His Cretan fight, the conquered Minotaur:
The soldiers shout around with generous rage,
And in that victory their own presage.
He praised their ardour, inly pleased to see
His host the flower of Grecian chivalry.   120
All day he marched, and all the ensuing night,
And saw the city with returning light.
The process of the war I need not tell,
How Theseus conquered, and how Creon fell;
Or after, how by storm the walls were won,   125
Or how the victor sacked and burned the town;
How to the ladies he restored again
The bodies of their lords in battle slain;
And with what ancient rites they were interred;

All these to fitter time shall be deferred: 130
I spare the widows' tears, their woful cries,
And howling at their husbands' obsequies;
How Theseus at these funerals did assist,
And with what gifts the mourning dames dismissed.
    Thus when the victor chief had Creon slain,   135
And conquered Thebes, he pitched upon the plain
His mighty camp, and when the day returned,
The country wasted and the hamlets burned,
And left the pillagers, to rapine bred,
Without control to strip and spoil the dead.   140
    There, in a heap of slain, among the rest
Two youthful knights they found beneath a load oppressed
Of slaughtered foes, whom first to death they sent,
The trophies of their strength, a bloody monument.
Both fair, and both of royal blood they seemed,   145
Whom kinsmen to the crown the heralds deemed;
That day in equal arms they fought for fame;
Their swords, their shields, their surcoats were the same.
Close by each other laid they pressed the ground,
Their manly bosoms pierced with many a grisly wound; 150
Nor well alive nor wholly dead they were,
But some faint signs of feeble life appear:
The wandering breath was on the wing to part,
Weak was the pulse, and hardly heaved the heart.
These two were sisters' sons; and Arcite one,   155
Much famed in fields, with valiant Palamon.
From these their costly arms the spoilers rent,
And softly both conveyed to Theseus' tent:
Whom, known of Creon's line, and cured with care,
He to his city sent as prisoners of the war;   160
Hopeless of ransom, and condemned to lie
In durance, doomed a lingering death to die.
    This done, he marched away with warlike sound,
And to his Athens turned with laurels crowned,

Where happy long he lived, much loved, and more re-
 nowned.   165
But in a tower, and never to be loosed,
The woful captive kinsmen are enclosed.
 Thus year by year they pass, and day by day,
Till once ('twas on the morn of cheerful May)
The young Emilia, fairer to be seen   170
Than the fair lily on the flowery green,
More fresh than May herself in blossoms new
(For with the rosy colour strove her hue),
Waked, as her custom was, before the day,
To do the observance due to sprightly May; 175
For sprightly May commands our youth to keep
The vigils of her night, and breaks their sluggard sleep;
Each gentle breast with kindly warmth she moves;
Inspires new flames, revives extinguished loves.
In this remembrance, Emily ere day   180
Arose, and dressed herself in rich array;
Fresh as the month, and as the morning fair;
Adown her shoulders fell her length of hair;
A ribband did the braided tresses bind,
The rest was loose, and wantoned in the wind: 185
Aurora had but newly chased the night,
And purpled o'er the sky with blushing light,
When to the garden-walk she took her way,
To sport and trip along in cool of day,
And offer maiden vows in honour of the May. 190
 At every turn she made a little stand,
And thrust among the thorns her lily hand
To draw the rose; and every rose she drew,
She shook the stalk, and brushed away the dew;
Then party-coloured flowers of white and red 195
She wove, to make a garland for her head;
This done, she sung and carolled out so clear,
That men and angels might rejoice to hear; .

Even wondering Philomel forgot to sing,
And learned from her to welcome in the spring.   200
The tower, of which before was mention made,
Within whose keep the captive knights were laid,
Built of a large extent, and strong withal,
Was one partition of the palace wall;
The garden was enclosed within the square,   205
Where young Emilia took the morning air.
It happened Palamon, the prisoner knight,
Restless for woe, arose before the light,
And with his jailer's leave desired to breathe
An air more wholesome than the damps beneath.   210
This granted, to the tower he took his way,
Cheered with the promise of a glorious day;
Then cast a languishing regard around,
And saw with hateful eyes the temples crowned
With golden spires, and all the hostile ground.   215
He sighed, and turned his eyes, because he knew
'Twas but a larger jail he had in view;
Then looked below, and from the castle's height
Beheld a nearer and more pleasing sight:
The garden, which before he had not seen,   220
In spring's new livery clad of white and green,
Fresh flowers in wide parterres, and shady walks between.
This viewed, but not enjoyed, with arms across
He stood, reflecting on his country's loss;
Himself an object of the public scorn,   225
And often wished he never had been born.
At last (for so his destiny required),
With walking giddy, and with thinking tired,
He through a little window cast his sight,
Though thick of bars, that gave a scanty light;   230
But even that glimmering served him to descry
The inevitable charms of Emily.
Scarce had he seen, but, seized with sudden smart,

Stung to the quick, he felt it at his heart;
Struck blind with overpowering light he stood,   235
Then started back amazed, and cried aloud.
   Young Arcite heard; and up he ran with haste,
To help his friend, and in his arms embraced;
And asked him why he looked so deadly wan,
And whence, and how, his change of cheer began?   240
Or who had done the offence? "But if," said he,
"Your grief alone is hard captivity,
For love of Heaven with patience undergo
A cureless ill, since Fate will have it so:
So stood our horoscope in chains to lie,   245
And Saturn in the dungeon of the sky,
Or other baleful aspect, ruled our birth,
When all the friendly stars were under earth;
Whate'er betides, by Destiny 'tis done;
And better bear like men than vainly seek to shun."   250
"Nor of my bonds," said Palamon again,
"Nor of unhappy planets I complain;
But when my mortal anguish caused my cry,
That moment I was hurt through either eye;
Pierced with a random shaft, I faint away,   255
And perish with insensible decay:
A glance of some new goddess gave the wound,
Whom, like Actæon, unaware I found.
Look how she walks along yon shady space!
Not Juno moves with more majestic grace,   260
And all the Cyprian queen is in her face.
If thou art Venus (for thy charms confess
That face was formed in heaven, nor art thou less,
Disguised in habit, undisguised in shape),
O help us captives from our chains to scape!   265
But if our doom be passed in bonds to lie
For life, and in a loathsome dungeon die,
Then be thy wrath appeased with our disgrace,

And show compassion to the Theban race,
Oppressed by tyrant power!"—While yet he spoke,   270
Arcite on Emily had fixed his look;
The fatal dart a ready passage found
And deep within his heart infixed the wound:
So that if Palamon were wounded sore,
Arcite was hurt as much as he or more: 275
Then from his inmost soul he sighed, and said,
"The beauty I behold has struck me dead:
Unknowingly she strikes, and kills by chance;
Poison is in her eyes, and death in every glance.
Oh, I must ask; nor ask alone, but move   280
Her mind to mercy, or must die for love."
    Thus Arcite; and thus Palamon replies
(Eager his tone, and ardent were his eyes):
"Speak'st thou in earnest, or in jesting vein?"
"Jesting," said Arcite, "suits but ill with pain."   285
"It suits far worse," said Palamon again,
And bent his brows, "with men who honour weigh,
Their faith to break, their friendship to betray;
But worst with thee, of noble lineage born,
My kinsman, and in arms my brother sworn.   290
Have we not plighted each our holy oath,
That one should be the common good of both;
One soul should both inspire, and neither prove
His fellow's hindrance in pursuit of love?
To this before the gods we gave our hands,   295
And nothing but our death can break the bands.
This binds thee, then, to farther my design,
As I am bound by vow to farther thine;
Nor canst, nor dar'st thou, traitor, on the plain
Appeach my honour, or thy own maintain,   300
Since thou art of my council, and the friend
Whose faith I trust, and on whose care depend.
And would'st thou court my lady's love, which I

Much rather than release, would choose to die?
But thou, false Arcite, never shalt obtain   305
Thy bad pretence; I told thee first my pain:
For first my love began ere thine was born;
Thou as my council, and my brother sworn,
Art bound to assist my eldership of right,
Or justly to be deemed a perjured knight."   310
    Thus Palamon; but Arcite with disdain
In haughty language thus replied again:
" Forsworn thyself: the traitor's odious name
I first return, and then disprove thy claim.
If love be passion, and that passion nursed   315
With strong desires, I loved the lady first.
Canst thou pretend desire, whom zeal inflamed
To worship, and a power celestial named?
Thine was devotion to the blest above,
I saw the woman, and desired her love;   320
First owned my passion, and to thee commend
The important secret, as my chosen friend.
Suppose (which yet I grant not) thy desire
A moment elder than my rival fire;
Can chance of seeing first thy title prove?   325
And know'st thou not, no law is made for love?
Law is to things which to free choice relate;
Love is not in our choice, but in our fate;
Laws are not positive; love's power we see
Is Nature's sanction, and her first decree.   330
Each day we break the bond of human laws
For love, and vindicate the common cause.
Laws for defence of civil rights are placed.
Love throws the fences down, and makes a general waste:
Maids, widows, wives without distinction fall;   335
The sweeping deluge, love, comes on, and covers all.
If then the laws of friendship I transgress,
I keep the greater, while I break the less;

And both are mad alike, since neither can possess;
Both hopeless to be ransomed, never more   340
To see the sun, but as he passes o'er.
Like Æsop's hounds contending for the bone:
Each pleaded right, and would be lord alone;
The fruitless fight continued all the day;
A cur came by and snatched the prize away.   345
As courtiers therefore justle for a grant,
And when they break their friendship, plead their want,
So thou, if Fortune will thy suit advance,
Love on, nor envy me my equal chance:
For I must love, and am resolved to try   350
My fate, or failing in the adventure die."
　　Great was their strife, which hourly was renewed,
Till each with mortal hate his rival viewed:
Now friends no more, nor walking hand in hand;
But when they met, they made a surly stand,   355
And glared like angry lions as they passed,
And wished that every look might be their last.
　　It chanced at length, Pirithous came to attend
This worthy Theseus, his familiar friend:
Their love in early infancy began,   360
And rose as childhood ripened into man,
Companions of the war, and loved so well,
That when one died, as ancient stories tell,
His fellow to redeem him went to hell.
　　But to pursue my tale: to welcome home   365
His warlike brother is Pirithous come:
Arcite of Thebes was known in arms long since,
And honoured by this young Thessalian prince.
Theseus, to gratify his friend and guest,
Who made our Arcite's freedom his request,   370
Restored to liberty the captive knight,
But on these hard conditions I recite:
That if hereafter Arcite should be found

Within the compass of Athenian ground,
By day or night, or on whate'er pretence,   375
His head should pay the forfeit of the offence.
To this Pirithous for his friend agreed,
And on his promise was the prisoner freed.
    Unpleased and pensive hence he takes his way,
At his own peril; for his life must pay.   380
Who now but Arcite mourns his bitter fate,
Finds his dear purchase, and repents too late?
"What have I gained," he said, "in prison pent,
If I but change my bonds for banishment?
And banished from her sight, I suffer more   385
In freedom than I felt in bonds before;
Forced from her presence, and condemned to live,
Unwelcome freedom, and unthanked reprieve:
Heaven is not but where Emily abides,
And where she's absent, all is hell besides.   390
Next to my day of birth, was that accursed
Which bound my friendship to Pirithous first:
Had I not known that prince, I still had been
In bondage, and had still Emilia seen:
For though I never can her grace deserve,   395
'Tis recompense enough to see and serve.
O Palamon, my kinsman and my friend,
How much more happy fates thy love attend!
Thine is the adventure, thine the victory,
Well has thy fortune turned the dice for thee: 400
Thou on that angel's face may'st feed thy eyes,
In prison, no; but blissful paradise!
Thou daily seest that sun of beauty shine,
And lov'st at least in love's extremest line.
I mourn in absence, love's eternal night;   405
And who can tell but since thou hast her sight,
And art a comely, young, and valiant knight,
Fortune (a various power) may cease to frown,

And by some ways unknown thy wishes crown?
But I, the most forlorn of human kind,   410
Nor help can hope, nor remedy can find;
But doomed to drag my loathsome life in care,
For my reward, must end it in despair.
Fire, water, air, and earth, and force of fates
That governs all, and heaven that all creates,   415
Nor art, nor Nature's hand can ease my grief;
Nothing but death, the wretch's last relief:
Then farewell youth, and all the joys that dwell
With youth and life, and life itself, farewell!
  " But why, alas! do mortal men in vain   420
Of Fortune, Fate, or Providence complain?
God gives us what he knows our wants require,
And better things than those which we desire:
Some pray for riches; riches they obtain;
But, watched by robbers, for their wealth are slain;   425
Some pray from prison to be freed; and come,
When guilty of their vows, to fall at home;
Murdered by those they trusted with their life,
A favoured servant, or a bosom wife.
Such dear-bought blessings happen every day,   430
Because we know not for what things to pray.
Like drunken sots about the streets we roam:
Well knows the sot he has a certain home,
Yet knows not how to find the uncertain place,
And blunders on, and staggers every pace.   435
Thus all seek happiness; but few can find,
For far the greater part of men are blind.
This is my case, who thought our utmost good
Was in one word of freedom understood:
The fatal blessing came: from prison free,   440
I starve abroad, and lose the sight of Emily.
  Thus Arcite; but if Arcite thus deplore
His sufferings, Palamon yet suffers more.

For when he knew his rival freed and gone,
He swells with wrath ; he makes outrageous moan ;   445
He frets, he fumes, he stares, he stamps the ground ;
The hollow tower with clamours rings around :
With briny tears he bathed his fettered feet,
And dropped all o'er with agony of sweat.
"Alas !" he cried, "I, wretch, in prison pine,   450
Too happy rival, while the fruit is thine :
Thou liv'st at large, thou draw'st thy native air,
Pleased with thy freedom, proud of my despair :
Thou mayst, since thou hast youth and courage joined,
A sweet behaviour and a solid mind,   455
Assemble ours, and all the Theban race,
To vindicate on Athens thy disgrace.
And after, by some treaty made, possess
Fair Emily, the pledge of lasting peace.
So thine shall be the beauteous prize, while I   460
Must languish in despair, in prison die.
Thus all the advantage of the strife is thine,
Thy portion double joys, and double sorrows mine."
    The rage of jealousy then fired his soul,
And his face kindled like a burning coal :   465
Now cold despair, succeeding in her stead,
To livid paleness turns the glowing red.
His blood, scarce liquid, creeps within his veins,
Like water which the freezing wind constrains.
Then thus he said : " Eternal Deities,   470
Who rule the world with absolute decrees,
And write whatever time shall bring to pass
With pens of adamant on plates of brass ;
What is the race of human kind your care
Beyond what all his fellow-creatures are ?   475
He with the rest is liable to pain,
And like the sheep, his brother-beast, is slain.
Cold, hunger, prisons, ills without a cure,

All these he must, and guiltless oft, endure;
Or does your justice, power, or prescience fail,   480
When the good suffer and the bad prevail ?
What worse to wretched virtue could befall,
If Fate or giddy Fortune governed all ?
Nay, worse than other beasts is our estate :
Them, to pursue their pleasures, you create;   485
We, bound by harder laws, must curb our will,
And your commands, not our desires, fulfil :
Then, when the creature is unjustly slain,
Yet, after death at least, he feels no pain;
But man, in life surcharged with woe before,   490
Not freed when dead, is doomed to suffer more.
A serpent shoots his sting at unaware;
An ambushed thief forelays a traveller;
The man lies murdered, while the thief and snake,
One gains the thickets, and one thrids the brake.   495
This let divines decide; but well I know,
Just or unjust, I have my share of woe:
Through Saturn seated in a luckless place,
And Juno's wrath that persecutes my race;
Or Mars and Venus in a quartil move   500
My pangs of jealousy for Arcite's love."
   Let Palamon oppressed in bondage mourn,
While to his exiled rival we return.
By this the sun, declining from his height,
The day had shortened to prolong the night: 505
The lengthened night gave length of misery,
Both to the captive lover and the free :
For Palamon in endless prison mourns,
And Arcite forfeits life if he returns;
The banished never hopes his love to see,   510
Nor hopes the captive lord his liberty.
'Tis hard to say who suffers greater pains;
One sees his love. but cannot break his chains;

One free, and all his motions uncontrolled,
Beholds whate'er he would but what he would behold.   515
Judge as you please, for I will haste to tell
What fortune to the banished knight befel.
When Arcite was to Thebes returned again,
The loss of her he loved renewed his pain ;
What could be worse than never more to see   520
His life, his soul, his charming Emily ?
He raved with all the madness of despair,
He roared, he beat his breast, he tore his hair.
Dry sorrow in his stupid eyes appears,
For wanting nourishment, he wanted tears :   525
His eyeballs in their hollow sockets sink,
Bereft of sleep ; he loathes his meat and drink ;
He withers at his heart, and looks as wan
As the pale spectre of a murdered man :
That pale turns yellow, and his face receives   530
The faded hue of sapless boxen leaves ;
In solitary groves he makes his moan,
Walks early out, and ever is alone ;
Nor, mixed in mirth, in youthful pleasure shares,
But sighs when songs and instruments he hears.   535
His spirits are so low, his voice is drowned ;
He hears as from afar, or in a swound,
Like the deaf murmurs of a distant sound :
Uncombed his locks, and squalid his attire,
Unlike the trim of love and gay desire ;   540
But full of museful mopings, which presage
The loss of reason and conclude in rage.
    This when he had endured a year or more,
Now wholly changed from what he was before,
It happened once, that, slumbering as he lay,   545
He dreamt (his dream began at break of day)
That Hermes o'er his head in air appeared,
And with soft words his drooping spirits cheered ;

His hat, adorned with wings, disclosed the god,
And in his hand he bore the sleep-compelling rod;   550
Such as he seemed, when, at his sire's command,
On Argus' head he laid the snaky wand.
"Arise," he said, "to conquering Athens go;
There Fate appoints an end of all thy woe."
The fright awakened Arcite with a start,   555
Against his bosom bounced his heaving heart;
But soon he said, with scarce recovered breath,
"And thither will I go to meet my death,
Sure to be slain; but death is my desire,
Since in Emilia's sight I shall expire."   560
By chance he spied a mirror while he spoke,
And gazing there beheld his altered look;
Wondering, he saw his features and his hue
So much were changed, that scarce himself he knew.
A sudden thought then starting in his mind,   565
"Since I in Arcite cannot Arcite find,
The world may search in vain with all their eyes,
But never penetrate through this disguise.
Thanks to the change which grief and sickness give,
In low estate I may securely live,   570
And see, unknown, my mistress day by day."
He said, and clothed himself in coarse array,
A labouring hind in show; then forth he went,
And to the Athenian towers his journey bent:
One squire attended in the same disguise,   575
Made conscious of his master's enterprise.
Arrived at Athens, soon he came to court,
Unknown, unquestioned in that thick resort;
Proffering for hire his service at the gate,
To drudge, draw water, and to run or wait.   580
    So fair befel him, that for little gain
He served at first Emilia's chamberlain;
And, watchful all advantages to spy,

Was still at hand, and in his master's eye;
And, as his bones were big, and sinews strong,   585
Refused no toil that could to slaves belong;
But from deep wells with engines water drew,
And used his noble hands the wood to hew.
He passed a year at least attending thus
On Emily, and called Philostratus.   590
But never was there man of his degree
So much esteemed, so well beloved as he.
So gentle of condition was he known,
That through the court his courtesy was blown:
All think him worthy of a greater place,   595
And recommend him to the royal grace;
That, exercised within a higher sphere,
His virtues more conspicuous might appear.
Thus by the general voice was Arcite praised,
And by great Theseus to high favour raised;   600
Among his menial servants first enrolled,
And largely entertained with sums of gold:
Besides what secretly from Thebes was sent,
Of his own income and his annual rent.
This well employed, he purchased friends and fame,   605
But cautiously concealed from whence it came.
Thus for three years he lived with large increase,
In arms of honour, and esteem in peace;
To Theseus' person he was ever near,
And Theseus for his virtues held him dear.   610

BOOK II.

WHILE Arcite lives in bliss, the story turns
Where hopeless Palamon in prison mourns.
For six long years immured, the captive knight
Had dragged his chains, and scarcely seen the light:
Lost liberty and love at once he bore;   5
His prison pained him much, his passion more:
Nor dares he hope his fetters to remove,
Nor ever wishes to be free from love.
    But when the sixth revolving year was run,
And May within the Twins received the sun,   10
Were it by Chance, or forceful Destiny,
Which forms in causes first whate'er shall be,
Assisted by a friend one moonless night,
This Palamon from prison took his flight:
A pleasant beverage he prepared before   15
Of wine and honey mixed, with added store
Of opium; to his keeper this he brought,
Who swallowed unaware the sleepy draught,
And snored secure till morn, his senses bound
In slumber, and in long oblivion drowned.   20
Short was the night, and careful Palamon
Sought the next covert ere the rising sun.
A thick-spread forest near the city lay;
To this with lengthened strides he took his way
(For far he could not fly, and feared the day);   25
Safe from pursuit, he meant to shun the light,
Till the brown shadows of the friendly night
To Thebes might favour his intended flight.
When to his country come, his next design
Was all the Theban race in arms to join,   30
And war on Theseus, till he lost his life,
Or won the beauteous Emily to wife.

Thus while his thoughts the lingering day beguile,
To gentle Arcite let us turn our style ;
Who little dreamt how nigh he was to care,   35
Till treacherous fortune caught him in the snare.
The morning lark, the messenger of day,
Saluted in her song the morning gray ;
And soon the sun arose with beams so bright,
That all the horizon laughed to see the joyous sight.   40
He with his tepid rays the rose renews,
And licks the dropping leaves, and dries the dews ;
When Arcite left his bed, resolved to pay
Observance to the month of merry May :
Forth on his fiery steed betimes he rode,   45
That scarcely prints the turf on which he trod ;
At ease he seemed, and, prancing o'er the plains,
Turned only to the grove his horse's reins,
The grove I named before ; and, lighting there,
A woodbine garland sought to crown his hair ;   50
Then turned his face against the rising day,
And raised his voice to welcome in the May :
   " For thee, sweet month, the groves green liveries wear,
If not the first, the fairest of the year :
For thee the Graces lead the dancing hours,   55
And Nature's ready pencil paints the flowers :
When thy short reign is past, the feverish sun
The sultry tropic fears, and moves more slowly on.
So may thy tender blossoms fear no blight,
Nor goats with venomed teeth thy tendrils bite,   60
As thou shalt guide my wandering feet to find
The fragrant greens I seek, my brows to bind."
   His vows addressed, within the grove he strayed,
Till Fate, or Fortune, near the place conveyed
His steps where secret Palamon was laid.   65
Full little thought of him the gentle knight,
Who, flying death, had there concealed his flight,

In brakes and brambles hid, and shunning mortal sight:
And less he knew him for his hated foe,
But feared him as a man he did not know.   70
But as it has been said of ancient years,
That fields are full of eyes and woods have ears;
For this the wise are ever on their guard,
For unforeseen, they say, is unprepared.
Uncautious Arcite thought himself alone,   75
And less than all suspected Palamon,
Who, listening, heard him, while he searched the grove,
And loudly sung his roundelay of love:
But on the sudden stopped, and silent stood,
As lovers often muse, and change their mood;   80
Now high as heaven, and then as low as hell,
Now up, now down, as buckets in a well;
For Venus, like her day, will change her cheer,
And seldom shall we see a Friday clear.
Thus Arcite having sung, with altered hue   85
Sunk on the ground, and from his bosom drew
A desperate sigh, accusing Heaven and Fate,
And angry Juno's unrelenting hate:
"Cursed be the day when first I did appear!
Let it be blotted from the calendar,   90
Lest it pollute the month, and poison all the year.
Still will the jealous queen pursue our race?
Cadmus is dead, the Theban city was:
Yet ceases not her hate; for all who come
From Cadmus are involved in Cadmus' doom.   95
I suffer for my blood: unjust decree,
That punishes another's crime on me.
In mean estate I serve my mortal foe,
The man who caused my country's overthrow.
This is not all; for Juno, to my shame,   100
Has forced me to forsake my former name;
Arcite I was, Philostratus I am.

That side of heaven is all my enemy:
Mars ruined Thebes; his mother ruined me.
Of all the royal race remains but one   105
Beside myself, the unhappy Palamon,
Whom Theseus holds in bonds and will not free;
Without a crime, except his kin to me.
Yet these, and all the rest, I could endure;
But love's a malady without a cure: 110
Fierce Love has pierced me with his fiery dart,
He fries within, and hisses at my heart.
Your eyes, fair Emily, my fate pursue;
I suffer for the rest, I die for you.
Of such a goddess no time leaves record,   115
Who burned the temple where she was adored:
And let it burn, I never will complain,
Pleased with my sufferings, if you knew my pain."
    At this a sickly qualm his heart assailed,
His ears ring inward, and his senses failed.   120
No word missed Palamon of all he spoke;
But soon to deadly pale he changed his look:
He trembled every limb, and felt a smart,
As if cold steel had glided through his heart;
No longer stayed, but starting from his place,   125
Discovered stood, and showed his hostile face:
    "False traitor, Arcite, traitor to thy blood,
Bound by thy sacred oath to seek my good,
Now art thou found forsworn for Emily,
And dar'st attempt her love, for whom I die.   130
So hast thou cheated Theseus with a wile,
Against thy vow, returning to beguile
Under a borrowed name: as false to me,
So false thou art to him who set thee free.
But rest assured, that either thou shalt die,   135
Or else renounce thy claim in Emily;
For though unarmed I am, and, freed by chance,

Am here without my sword or pointed lance,
Hope not, base man, unquestioned hence to go,
For I am Palamon, thy mortal foe."   140
   Arcite, who heard his tale and knew the man,
His sword unsheathed, and fiercely thus began :
"Now, by the gods who govern heaven above,
Wert thou not weak with hunger, mad with love,
That word had been thy last; or in this grove   145
This hand should force thee to renounce thy love;
The surety which I gave thee I defy :
Fool, not to know that love endures no tie,
And Jove but laughs at lovers' perjury.
Know, I will serve the fair in thy despite;   150
But, since thou art my kinsman and a knight,
Here, have my faith, to-morrow in this grove
Our arms shall plead the titles of our love :
And Heaven so help my right, as I alone
Will come, and keep the cause and quarrel both unknown,
With arms of proof, both for myself and thee ;   156
Choose thou the best, and leave the worst to me.
And, that at better ease thou mayst abide,
Bedding and clothes I will this night provide,
And needful sustenance, that thou mayst be   160
A conquest better won, and worthy me."
His promise Palamon accepts; but prayed
To keep it better than the first he made.
Thus fair they parted till the morrow's dawn ;
For each had laid his plighted faith to pawn.   165
Oh Love ! thou sternly dost thy power maintain,
And wilt not bear a rival in thy reign ;
Tyrants and thou all fellowship disdain.
This was in Arcite proved and Palamon :
Both in despair, yet each would love alone.   170
Arcite returned, and, as in honour tied,
His foe with bedding and with food supplied ;

Then, ere the day, two suits of armour sought,
Which, borne before him, on his steed he brought:
Both were of shining steel, and wrought so pure   175
As might the strokes of two such arms endure.
Now, at the time, and in the appointed place,
The challenger and challenged, face to face,
Approach; each other from afar they knew,
And from afar their hatred changed their hue.   180
So stands the Thracian herdsman with his spear,
Full in the gap, and hopes the hunted bear,
And hears him rustling in the wood, and sees
His course, at distance, by the bending trees:
And thinks, Here comes my mortal enemy,   185
And either he must fall in fight, or I:
This while he thinks, he lifts aloft his dart;
A generous chillness seizes every part,
The veins pour back the blood, and fortify the heart.
    Thus pale they meet; their eyes with fury burn;   190
None greets, for none the greeting will return;
But in dumb surliness each armed with care
His foe professed, as brother of the war;
Then both, no moment lost, at once advance
Against each other, armed with sword and lance: 195
They lash, they foin, they pass, they strive to bore
Their corselets, and the thinnest parts explore.
Thus two long hours in equal arms they stood,
And wounded, wound, till both were bathed in blood;
And not a foot of ground had either got,   200
As if the world depended on the spot.
Fell Arcite like an angry tiger fared,
And like a lion Palamon appeared:
Or as two boars whom love to battle draws,
With rising bristles and with frothy jaws;   205
Their adverse breasts with tusks oblique they wound;
With grunts and groans the forest rings around.

So fought the knights, and fighting must abide,
Till Fate an umpire sends their difference to decide.
The power that ministers to God's decrees,   210
And executes on earth what Heaven foresees,
Called Providence, or Chance, or fatal sway,
Comes with resistless force, and finds, or makes, her way.
Nor kings, nor nations, nor united power
One moment can retard the appointed hour;   215
And some one day, some wondrous chance appears,
Which happened not in centuries of years:
For sure, whate'er we mortals hate or love
Or hope or fear depends on powers above:
They move our appetites to good or ill,   220
And by foresight necessitate the will.
In Theseus this appears, whose youthful joy
Was beasts of chase in forests to destroy;
This gentle knight, inspired by jolly May,
Forsook his easy couch at early day,   225
And to the wood and wilds pursued his way.
Beside him rode Hippolyta the queen,
And Emily, attired in lively green,
With horns and hounds and all the tuneful cry,
To hunt a royal hart within the covert nigh: 230
And, as he followed Mars before, so now
He serves the goddess of the silver bow.
The way that Theseus took was to the wood,
Where the two knights in cruel battle stood:
The laund on which they fought, the appointed place   235
In which the uncoupled hounds began the chase.
Thither forth-right he rode to rouse the prey,
That, shaded by the fern, in harbour lay,
And thence dislodged, was wont to leave the wood
For open fields, and cross the crystal flood;   240
Approached, and looking underneath the sun,
He saw proud Arcite and fierce Palamon,

In mortal battle doubling blow on blow;
Like lightning flamed their falchions to and fro,
And shot a dreadful gleam; so strong they strook,   245
There seemed less force required to fell an oak.
He gazed with wonder on their equal might,
Looked eager on, but knew not either knight.
Resolved to learn, he spurred his fiery steed
With goring rowels to provoke his speed.   250
The minute ended that began the race,
So soon he was betwixt them on the place;
And, with his sword unsheathed, on pain of life
Commands both combatants to cease their strife;
Then with imperious tone pursues his threat: 255
"What are you? why in arms together met?
How dares your pride presume against my laws
As in a listed field to fight your cause,
Unasked the royal grant; no marshal by,
As knightly rites require, nor judge to try?"   260
Then Palamon, with scarce recovered breath,
Thus hasty spoke: "We both deserve the death,
And both would die; for'look the world around,
A pair so wretched is not to be found.
Our life's a load; encumbered with the charge,   265
We long to set the imprisoned soul at large.
Now, as thou art a sovereign judge, decree
The rightful doom of death to him and me;
Let neither find thy grace, for grace is cruelty.
Me first, oh, kill me first, and cure my woe!   270
Then sheath the sword of justice on my foe;
Or kill him first, for when his name is heard,
He foremost will receive his due reward.
Arcite of Thebes is he, thy mortal foe,
On whom thy grace did liberty bestow;   275
But first contracted, that, if ever found
By day or night upon the Athenian ground,

His head should pay the forfeit; see returned
The perjured knight, his oath and honour scorned:
For this is he, who, with a borrowed name   280
And proffered service, to thy palace came,
Now called Philostratus; retained by thee,
A traitor trusted, and in high degree,
Aspiring to the bed of beauteous Emily.
My part remains: from Thebes my birth I own,   285
And call myself the unhappy Palamon.
Think me not like that man; since no disgrace
Can force me to renounce the honour of my race.
Know me for what I am: I broke thy chain,
Nor promised I thy prisoner to remain: 290
The love of liberty with life is given,
And life itself the inferior gift of heaven.
Thus without crime I fled; but farther know,
I, with this Arcite, am thy mortal foe:
Then give me death, since I thy life pursue;   295
For safeguard of thyself, death is my due.
More wouldst thou know? I love bright Emily,
And for her sake and in her sight will die:
But kill my rival too, for he no less
Deserves; and I thy righteous doom will bless,   300
Assured that what I lose he never shall possess."
To this replied the stern Athenian prince,
And sourly smiled: "In owning your offence
You judge yourself, and I but keep record
In place of law, while you pronounce the word.   305
Take your desert, the death you have decreed;
I seal your doom, and ratify the deed:
By Mars, the patron of my arms, you die."
    He said; dumb sorrow seized the standers-by.
The queen, above the rest, by nature good   310
(The pattern formed of perfect womanhood),
For tender pity wept: when she began,

Through the bright quire the infectious virtue ran.
All dropped their tears, even the contended maid;
And thus among themselves they softly said: 315
"What eyes can suffer this unworthy sight!
Two youths of royal blood, renowned in fight,
The mastership of heaven in face and mind,
And lovers, far beyond their faithless kind:
See their wide streaming wounds; they neither came   320
From pride of empire nor desire of fame:
Kings fight for kingdoms, madmen for applause;
But love for love alone, that crowns the lover's cause."
This thought, which ever bribes the beauteous kind,
Such pity wrought in every lady's mind,   325
They left their steeds, and prostrate on the place,
From the fierce king implored the offenders' grace.

He paused a while, stood silent in his mood
(For yet his rage was boiling in his blood);
But soon his tender mind the impression felt.   330
(As softest metals are not slow to melt
And pity soonest runs in gentle minds.)
Then reasons with himself; and first he finds
His passion cast a mist before his sense,
And either made or magnified the offence.   335
Offence! Of what? To whom? Who judged the cause?
The prisoner freed himself by Nature's laws;
Born free, he sought his right; the man he freed
Was perjured, but his love excused the deed:
Thus pondering, he looked under with his eyes,   340
And saw the women's tears, and heard their cries,
Which moved compassion more; he shook his head,
And softly sighing to himself he said:

"Curse on the unpardoning prince, whom tears can draw
To no remorse, who rules by lion's law;   345
And, deaf to prayers, by no submission bowed,
Rends all alike, the penitent and proud!"

At this with look serene he raised his head;
Reason resumed her place, and passion fled.
Then thus aloud he spoke: "The power of Love,   350
In earth, and seas, and air, and heaven above,
Rules, unresisted, with an awful nod,
By daily miracles declared a god;
He blinds the wise, gives eyesight to the blind;
And moulds and stamps anew the lover's mind.   355
Behold that Arcite, and this Palamon,
Freed from my fetters, and in safety gone,
What hindered either in their native soil
At ease to reap the harvest of their toil?
But Love, their lord, did otherwise ordain,   360
And brought them, in their own despite again,
To suffer death deserved; for well they know
'Tis in my power, and I their deadly foe.
The proverb holds, that to be wise and love,
Is hardly granted to the gods above.   365
See how the madmen bleed! behold the gains
With which their master, Love, rewards their pains!
For seven long years, on duty every day,
Lo! their obedience, and their monarch's pay!
Yet, as in duty bound, they serve him on;   370
And, ask the fools, they think it wisely done;
Nor ease nor wealth nor life itself regard;
For 'tis their maxim, love is love's reward.
This is not all: the fair, for whom they strove,
Nor knew before, nor could suspect their love,   375
Nor thought, when she beheld the fight from far,
Her beauty was the occasion of the war.
But sure a general doom on man is passed,
And all are fools and lovers, first or last:
This, both by others and myself, I know,   380
For I have served their sovereign long ago;
Oft have been caught within the winding train

Of female snares, and felt the lover's pain,
And learned how far the god can human hearts constrain.
To this remembrance, and the prayers of those   385
Who for the offending warriors interpose,
I give their forfeit lives, on this accord,
To do me homage as their sovereign lord;
And as my vassals, to their utmost might,
Assist my person and assert my right."   390
This freely sworn, the knights their grace obtained;
Then thus the king his secret thought explained:
"If wealth, or honour, or a royal race,
Or each, or all, may win a lady's grace,
Then either of you knights may well deserve   395
A princess born; and such is she you serve:
For Emily is sister to the crown,
And but too well to both her beauty known.
But should you combat till you both were dead,
Two lovers cannot share a single bed.   400
As, therefore, both are equal in degree,
The lot of both be left to destiny.
Now hear the award, and happy may it prove
To her, and him who best deserves her love.
Depart from hence in peace, and free as air,   405
Search the wide world, and where you please repair:
But on the day when this returning sun
To the same point through every sign has run,
Then each of you his hundred knights shall bring
In royal lists, to fight before the king;   410
And then the knight, whom Fate or happy Chance
Shall with his friends to victory advance,
And grace his arms so far in equal fight,
From out the bars to force his opposite,
Or kill, or make him recreant on the plain,   415
The prize of valour and of love shall gain;
The vanquished party shall their claim release,

And the long jars conclude in lasting peace.
The charge be mine to adorn the chosen ground,
The theatre of war, for champions so renownèd;			420
And take the patron's place of either knight,
With eyes impartial to behold the fight;
And Heaven of me so judge as I shall judge aright.
If both are satisfied with this accord,
Swear by the laws of knighthood on my sword."			425
    Who now but Palamon exults with joy?
And ravished Arcite seems to touch the sky.
The whole assembled troop was pleased as well,
Extolled the award, and on their knees they fell
To bless the gracious king. The knights, with leave			430
Departing from the place, his last commands receive;
On Emily with equal ardour look,
And from her eyes their inspiration took.
From thence to Thebes' old walls pursue their way,
Each to provide his champions for the day.			435
    It might be deemed, on our historian's part,
Or too much negligence, or want of art,
If he forgot the vast magnificence
Of royal Theseus, and his large expense.
He first enclosed for lists a level ground,			440
The whole circumference a mile around;
The form was circular; and all without
A trench was sunk, to moat the place about.
Within, an amphitheatre appeared,
Raised in degrees, to sixty paces reared:			445
That when a man was placed in one degree,
Height was allowed for him above to see.
    Eastward was built a gate of marble white
The like adorned the western opposite.
A nobler object than this fabric was			450
Rome never saw, nor of so vast a space:
For, rich with spoils of many a conquered land,

All arts and artists Theseus could command,
Who sold for hire, or wrought for better fame;
The master-painters and the carvers came.   455
So rose within the compass of the year
An age's work, a glorious theatre.
Then o'er its eastern gate was raised above
A temple, sacred to the Queen of Love;
An altar stood below; on either hand   460
A priest with roses crowned, who held a myrtle wand.
   The dome of Mars was on the gate opposed,
And on the north a turret was enclosed
Within the wall, of alabaster white
And crimson coral, for the Queen of Night,   465
Who takes in sylvan sports her chaste delight.
   Within these oratories might you see
Rich carvings, portraitures, and imagery;
Where every figure to the life expressed
The godhead's power to whom it was addressed.   470
In Venus' temple on the sides were seen
The broken slumbers of enamoured men;
Prayers that even spoke, and pity seemed to call,
And issuing sighs that smoked along the wall;
Complaints and hot desires, the lover's hell,   475
And scalding tears that wore a channel where they fell;
And all around were nuptial bonds, the ties
Of love's assurance, and a train of lies,
That, made in lust, conclude in perjuries;
Beauty, and Youth, and Wealth, and Luxury,   480
And sprightly Hope, and short-enduring Joy,
And Sorceries, to raise the infernal powers,
And Sigils framed in planetary hours;
Expense, and After-thought, and idle Care,
And Doubts of motley hue, and dark Despair;   485
Suspicions, and fantastical Surmise,
And Jealousy suffused, with jaundice in her eyes,

Discolouring all she viewed, in tawny dressed,
Down-looked, and with a cuckow on her fist.
Opposed to her, on the other side advance   490
The costly feast, the carol, and the dance,
Minstrels and music, poetry and play,
And balls by night, and tournaments by day.
All these were painted on the wall, and more;
With acts and monuments of times before,   495
And others added by prophetic doom,
And lovers yet unborn, and loves to come:
For there the Idalian mount and Citheron,
The court of Venus, was in colours drawn;
Before the palace gate, in careless dress   500
And loose array, sat portress Idleness;
There, by the fount, Narcissus pined alone;
There Samson was, with wiser Solomon,
And all the mighty names by love undone.
Medea's charms were there; Circean feasts,   505
With bowls that turned enamoured youths to beasts.
Here might be seen, that beauty, wealth, and wit,
And prowess to the power of love submit;
The spreading snare for all mankind is laid,
And lovers all betray, and are betrayed.   510
The goddess' self some noble hand had wrought;
Smiling she seemed, and full of pleasing thought;
From ocean as she first began to rise,
And smoothed the ruffled seas, and cleared the skies;
She trod the brine, all bare below the breast,   515
And the green waves but ill concealed the rest:
A lute she held; and on her head was seen
A wreath of roses red and myrtles green;
Her turtles fanned the buxom air above;
And by his mother stood an infant Love,   520
With wings unfledged; his eyes were banded o'er,
His hands a bow, his back a quiver bore,

Supplied with arrows bright and keen, a deadly store.

But in the dome of mighty Mars the red

With different figures all the sides were spread ;   525

This temple, less in form, with equal grace,

Was imitative of the first in Thrace ;

For that cold region was the loved abode

And sovereign mansion of the warrior god.

The landscape was a forest wide and bare,   530

Where neither beast nor human kind repair ;

The fowl that scent afar the borders fly,

And shun the bitter blast, and wheel about the sky.

A cake of scurf lies baking on the ground,

And prickly stubs, instead of trees, are found ;   535

Or woods with knots and knares deformed and old, ,

Headless the most, and hideous to behold ;

A rattling tempest through the branches went,

That stripped them bare, and one sole way they bent.

Heaven froze above severe, the clouds congeal,   540

And through the crystal vault appeared the standing hail.

Such was the face without : a mountain stood

Threatening from high, and overlooked the wood :

Beneath the lowering brow, and on a bent,

The temple stood of Mars armipotent ;   545

The frame of burnished steel, that cast a glare

From far, and seemed to thaw the freezing air.

A straight long entry to the temple led,

Blind with high walls, and horror over head ;

Thence issued such a blast and hollow roar   550

As threatened from the hinge to heave the door ;

In through that door a northern light there shone ;

'Twas all it had, for windows there were none.

The gate was adamant; eternal frame !

Which, hewed by Mars himself, from Indian quarries came,

The labour of a god; and all along   555

Tough iron plates were clenched to make it strong.

A tun about was every pillar there;
A polished mirror shone not half so clear.
There saw I how the secret felon wrought,　　560
And treason labouring in the traitor's thought,
And midwife Time the ripened plot to murder brought.
There the red Anger dared the pallid Fear;
Next stood Hypocrisy, with holy leer,
Soft, smiling, and demurely looking down,　　565
But hid the dagger underneath the gown;
The assassinating wife the household fiend;
And, far the blackest there, the traitor-friend.
On the other side there stood Destruction bare,
Unpunished Rapine, and a waste of war;　　570
Contest with sharpened knives in cloisters drawn,
And all with blood bespread the holy lawn.
Loud menaces were heard, and foul disgrace,
And bawling infamy, in language base;
Till sense was lost in sound, and silence fled the place.　　575
The slayer of himself yet saw I there,
The gore congealed was clotted in his hair;
With eyes half closed and gaping mouth he lay,
And grim as when he breathed his sullen soul away.
In midst of all the dome, Misfortune sate,　　580
And gloomy Discontent, and fell Debate,
And Madness laughing in his ireful mood;
And armed Complaint on theft; and cries of blood.
There was the murdered corpse, in covert laid,
And violent death in thousand shapes displayed;　　585
The city to the soldier's rage resigned;
Successless wars, and poverty behind:
Ships burnt in fight, or forced on rocky shores,
And the rash hunter strangled by the boars:
The new-born babe by nurses overlaid;　　590
And the cook caught within the raging fire he made.
All ills of Mars his nature, flame and steel:

The gasping charioteer beneath the wheel
Of his own car; the ruined house that falls
And intercepts her lord betwixt the walls: 595
The whole division that to Mars pertains,
All trades of death that deal in steel for gains
Were there: the butcher, armourer, and smith,
Who forges sharpened falchions, or the scythe.
The scarlet conquest on a tower was placed,   600
With shouts and soldiers' acclamations graced:
A pointed sword hung threatening o'er his head,
Sustained but by a slender twine of thread.
There saw I Mars his ides, the Capitol,
The seer in vain foretelling Cæsar's fall;   605
The last triumvirs, and the wars they move,
And Antony, who lost the world for love.
These, and a thousand more, the fane adorn;
Their fates were painted ere the men were born,
All copied from the heavens, and ruling force   610
Of the red star, in his revolving course.
The form of Mars high on a chariot stood,
All sheathed in arms, and gruffly looked the god;
Two geomantic figures were displayed
Above his head, a warrior and a maid,   615
One when direct, and one when retrograde.
    Tired with deformities of death, I haste
To the third temple of Diana chaste.
A sylvan scene with various greens was drawn,
Shades on the sides, and on the midst a lawn;   620
The silver Cynthia, with her nymphs around,
Pursued the flying deer, the woods with horns resound:
Calisto there stood manifest of shame,
And, turned a bear, the northern star became:
Her son was next, and, by peculiar grace,   625
In the cold circle held the second place;
The stag Actæon in the stream had spied

The naked huntress, and for seeing died;
His hounds, unknowing of his change, pursue
The chase, and their mistaken master slew.   630
Peneian Daphne, too, was there to see,
Apollo's love before, and now his tree.
The adjoining fane the assembled Greeks expressed,
And hunting of the Calydonian beast;
Œnides' valour, and his envied prize;   635
The fatal power of Atalanta's eyes;
Diana's vengeance on the victor shown,
The murderess mother, and consuming son;
The Volscian queen extended on the plain,
The treason punished, and the traitor slain.   640
The rest were various huntings, well designed,
And savage beasts destroyed, of every kind.
The graceful goddess was arrayed in green;
About her feet were little beagles seen,
That watched with upward eyes the motions of their queen.
Her legs were buskined, and the left before,   646
In act to shoot; a silver bow she bore,
And at her back a painted quiver wore.
She trod a wexing moon, that soon would wane,
And, drinking borrowed light, be filled again;   650
With downcast eyes, as seeming to survey
The dark dominions, her alternate sway.
Before her stood a woman in her throes,
And called Lucina's aid, her burden to disclose.
All these the painter drew with such command,   655
That Nature snatched the pencil from his hand,
Ashamed and angry that his art could feign,
And mend the tortures of a mother's pain.
Theseus beheld the fanes of every god,
And thought his mighty cost was well bestowed.   660
So princes now their poets should regard;
But few can write, and fewer can reward.

The theatre thus raised, the lists enclosed,
And all with vast magnificence disposed,
We leave the monarch pleased, and haste to bring   665
The knights to combat, and their arms to sing.

BOOK III.

THE day approached when Fortune should decide
The important enterprise, and give the bride;
For now the rivals round the world had sought,
And each his number, well appointed, brought.
The nations far and near contend in choice,   5
And send the flower of war by public voice;
That after or before were never known
Such chiefs, as each an army seemed alone:
Beside the champions, all of high degree,
Who knighthood loved, and deeds of chivalry,   10
Thronged to the lists, and envied to behold
The names of others, not their own, enrolled.
Nor seems it strange; for every noble knight,
Who loves the fair, and is endued with might,
In such a quarrel would be proud to fight.   15
There breathes not scarce a man on British ground
(An isle for love and arms of old renowned)
But would have sold his life to purchase fame,
To Palamon or Arcite sent his name;
And had the land selected of the best,   20
Half had come hence, and let the world provide the rest.
A hundred knights with Palamon there came,
Approved in fight, and men of mighty name;
Their arms were several, as their nations were,
But furnished all alike with sword and spear.   25
Some wore coat armour, imitating scale,
And next their skins were stubborn shirts of mail;
Some wore a breastplate and a light juppon,
Their horses clothed with rich caparison;
Some for defence would leathern bucklers use   30
Of folded hides, and others shields of Pruce.
One hung a pole-axe at his saddle-bow,

And one a heavy mace to stun the foe;
One for his legs and knees provided well,
With jambeux armed, and double plates of steel;   35
This on his helmet wore a lady's glove,
And that a sleeve embroidered by his love.
   With Palamon above the rest in place,
Lycurgus came, the surly king of Thrace;
Black was his beard, and manly was his face: 40
The balls of his broad eyes rolled in his head,
And glared betwixt a yellow and a red;
He looked a lion with a gloomy stare,
And o'er his eyebrows hung his matted hair;
Big-boned and large of limbs, with sinews strong,   45
Broad-shouldered, and his arms were round and long.
Four milk-white bulls (the Thracian use of old)
Were yoked to draw his car of burnished gold.
Upright he stood, and bore aloft his shield,
Conspicuous from afar, and overlooked the field.   50
His surcoat was a bear-skin on his back;
His hair hung long behind, and glossy raven-black.
His ample forehead bore a coronet,
With sparkling diamonds and with rubies set.
Ten brace, and more, of greyhounds, snowy fair,   55
And tall as stags, ran loose, and coursed around his chair,
A match for pards in flight, in grappling for the bear;
With golden muzzles all their mouths were bound,
And collars of the same their necks surround.
Thus through the fields Lycurgus took his way;   60
His hundred knights attend in pomp and proud array.
   To match this monarch, with strong Arcite came
Emetrius, king of Inde, a mighty name!
On a bay courser, goodly to behold,
The trappings of his horse embossed with barbarous gold.   65
Not Mars bestrode a steed with greater grace;
His surcoat o'er his arms was cloth of Thrace,

Adorned with pearls, all orient, round, and great;
His saddle was of gold, with emeralds set;
His shoulders large a mantle did attire,   70
With rubies thick, and sparkling as the fire;
His amber-coloured locks in ringlets run,
With graceful negligence, and shone against the sun.
His nose was aquiline, his eyes were blue,
Ruddy his lips, and fresh and fair his hue;   75
Some sprinkled freckles on his face were seen,
Whose dusk set off the whiteness of the skin.
His awful presence did the crowd surprise,
Nor durst the rash spectator meet his eyes;
Eyes that confessed him born for kingly sway,   80
So fierce, they flashed intolerable day.
His age in nature's youthful prime appeared,
And just began to bloom his yellow beard.
Whene'er he spoke, his voice was heard around,
Loud as a trumpet, with a silver sound;   85
A laurel wreathed his temples, fresh and green,
And myrtle sprigs, the marks of love, were mixed between.
Upon his fist he bore, for his delight,
An eagle well reclaimed, and lily white.
    His hundred knights attend him to the war,   90
All armed for battle; save their heads were bare.
Words and devices blazed on every shield,
And pleasing was the terror of the field.
For kings, and dukes, and barons you might see,
Like sparkling stars, though different in degree,   95
All for the increase of arms, and love of chivalry.
Before the king tame leopards led the way,
And troops of lions innocently play.
So Bacchus through the conquered Indies rode,
And beasts in gambols frisked before their honest god.   100
    In this array, the war of either side
Through Athens passed with military pride.

At prime they entered on the Sunday morn;
Rich tapestry spread the streets, and flowers the pots adorn.
The town was all a jubilee of feasts;   105
So Theseus willed in honour of his guests;
Himself with open arms the kings embraced,
Then all the rest in their degrees were graced.
No harbinger was needful for the night,
For every house was proud to lodge a knight.   110
    I pass the royal treat, nor must relate
The gifts bestowed, nor how the champions sate;
Who first, who last, or how the knights addressed
Their vows, or who was the fairest at the feast;
Whose voice, whose graceful dance did most surprise;   115
Soft amorous sighs, and silent love of eyes.
The rivals call my Muse another way,
To sing their vigils for the ensuing day.
    'Twas ebbing darkness, past the noon of night,
And Phosphor, on the confines of the light,   120
Promised the sun; ere day began to spring,
The tuneful lark already stretched her wing,
And flickering on her nest, made short essays to sing,
When wakeful Palamon, preventing day,
Took to the royal lists his early way,   125
To Venus at her fane, in her own house, to pray.
There, falling on his knees before her shrine,
He thus implored with prayers her power divine;
" Creator Venus, genial power of love,
The bliss of men below, and gods above!   130
Beneath the sliding sun thou runn'st thy race,
Dost fairest shine, and best become thy place.
For thee the winds their eastern blasts forbear,
Thy month reveals the spring, and opens all the year.
Thee, Goddess, thee the storms of winter fly;   135
Earth smiles with flowers renewing, laughs the sky,
And birds to lays of love their tuneful notes apply.

For thee the lion loathes the taste of blood,
And roaring hunts his female through the wood;
For thee the bulls rebellow through the groves,   140
And tempt the stream, and snuff their absent loves.
'Tis thine, whate'er is pleasant, good, or fair;
All nature is thy province, life thy care;
Thou mad'st the world, and dost the world repair.
Thou gladder of the mount of Cytheron,   145
Increase of Jove, companion of the sun,
If e'er Adonis touched thy tender heart,
Have pity, Goddess, for thou know'st the smart!
Alas! I have not words to tell my grief;
To vent my sorrow would be some relief;   150
Light sufferings give us leisure to complain;
We groan, but cannot speak, in greater pain.
O Goddess, tell thyself what I would say!
Thou know'st it, and I feel too much to pray.
So grant my suit, as I enforce my might,   155
In love to be thy champion and thy knight,
A servant to thy sex, a slave to thee,
A foe professed to barren chastity;
Nor ask I fame or honour of the field,
Nor choose I more to vanquish than to yield: 160
In my divine Emilia make me blest,
Let fate or partial chance dispose the rest:
Find thou the manner, and the means prepare;
Possession, more than conquest, is my care.
Mars is the warrior's god; in him it lies   165
On whom he favours to confer the prize;
With smiling aspect you serenely move
In your fifth orb, and rule the realm of love.
The Fates but only spin the coarser clue,
The finest of the wool is left for you.   170
Spare me but one small portion of the twine,
And let the Sisters cut below your line:

The rest among the rubbish may they sweep,
Or add it to the yarn of some old miser's heap.
But if you this ambitious prayer deny   175
(A wish, I grant, beyond mortality),
Then let me sink beneath proud Arcite's arms,
And, I once dead, let him possess her charms."
  Thus ended he; then, with observance due,
The sacred incense on her altar threw :   180
The curling smoke mounts heavy from the fires;
At length it catches flame, and in a blaze expires;
At once the gracious Goddess gave the sign,
Her statue shook, and trembled all the shrine :
Pleased Palamon the tardy omen took;   185
For, since the flames pursued the trailing smoke,
He knew his boon was granted, but the day
To distance driven, and joy adjourned with long delay.
  Now morn with rosy light had streaked the sky,
Up rose the sun, and up rose Emily;   190
Addressed her early steps to Cynthia's fane,
In state attended by her maiden train,
Who bore the vests that holy rites require,
Incense, and odorous gums, and covered fire.
The plenteous horns with pleasant mead they crown,   195
Nor wanted aught besides in honour of the Moon.
Now, while the temple smoked with hallowed steam,
They wash the virgin in a living stream;
The secret ceremonies I conceal,
Uncouth, perhaps unlawful, to reveal :   200
But such they were as pagan use required,
Performed by women when the men retired,
Whose eyes profane their chaste mysterious rites
Might turn to scandal or obscene delights.
Well-meaners think no harm; but for the rest,   205
Things sacred they pervert, and silence is the best.
Her shining hair, uncombed, was loosely spread,

A crown of mastless oak adorned her head:
When to the shrine approached, the spotless maid
Had kindling fires on either altar laid   210
(The rites were such as were observed of old,
By Statius in his Theban story told),
Then kneeling with her hands across her breast,
Thus lowly she preferred her chaste request:
" O Goddess, haunter of the woodland green,   215
To whom both heaven and earth and seas are seen;
Queen of the nether skies, where half the year
Thy silver beams descend, and light the gloomy sphere:
Goddess of maids, and conscious of our hearts,
So keep me from the vengeance of thy darts   220
Which Niobe's devoted issue felt,
When hissing through the skies the feathered deaths were
      dealt :
As I desire to live a virgin life,
Nor know the name of mother or of wife.
Thy votress from my tender years I am,   225
And love, like thee, the woods and sylvan game.
Like death, thou know'st, I loathe the nuptial state,
And man, the tyrant of our sex, I hate,
A lowly servant, but a lofty mate ;
Where love is duty on the female side,   230
On theirs mere sensual gust, and sought with surly pride.
Now by thy triple shape, as thou art seen
In heaven, earth, hell, and everywhere a queen,
Grant this my first desire ; let discord cease,
And make betwixt the rivals lasting peace :   235
Quench their hot fire, or far from me remove
The flame, and turn it on some other love.
Or if my frowning stars have so decreed,
That one must be rejected, one succeed,
Make him my lord within whose faithful breast   240
Is fixed my image, and who loves me best.

But, oh! even that avert! I choose it not,
But take it as the least unhappy lot.
A maid I am, and of thy virgin train ;
Oh, let me still that spotless name retain !   245
Frequent the forests, thy chaste will obey,
And only make the beasts of chase my prey !"
   The flames ascend on either altar clear,
While thus the blameless maid addressed her prayer.
When lo! the burning fire that shone so bright   250
Flew off, all sudden, with extinguished light,
And left one altar dark, a little space,
Which turned self-kindled, and renewed the blaze ;
That other victor-flame a moment stood,
Then fell, and lifeless left the extinguished wood ;   255
For ever lost, the irrevocable light
Forsook the blackening coals, and sunk to night :
At either end it whistled as it flew,
And as the brands were green, so dropped the dew,
Infected as it fell with sweat of sanguine hue.   260
   The maid from that ill omen turned her eyes,
And with loud shrieks and clamours rent the skies;
Nor knew what signified the boding sign,
But found the powers displeased, and feared the wrath
    divine.
Then shook the sacred shrine, and sudden light   265
Sprung through the vaulted roof, and made the temple bright,
The Power, behold! the Power in glory shone,
By her bent bow and her keen arrows known ;
The rest, a huntress issuing from the wood,
Reclining on her cornel spear she stood.   270
Then gracious thus began : "Dismiss thy fear,
And Heaven's unchanged decrees attentive hear :
More powerful gods have torn thee from my side,
Unwilling to resign, and doomed a bride ;
The two contending knights are weighed above ;   275

One Mars protects, and one the Queen of Love:
But which the man is in the Thunderer's breast,
This he pronounced, '''Tis he who loves thee best.'
The fire that, once extinct, revived again
Foreshows the love allotted to remain.   280
Farewell!" she said, and vanished from the place;
The sheaf of arrows shook, and rattled in the case.
Aghast at this, the royal virgin stood,
Disclaimed, and now no more a sister of the wood:
But to the parting goddess thus she prayed: 285
"Propitious still, be present to my aid,
Nor quite abandon your once favoured maid."
Then sighing she returned; but smiled betwixt,
With hopes, and fears, and joys with sorrows mixed.
    The next returning planetary hour   290
Of Mars, who shared the heptarchy of power,
His steps bold Arcite to the temple bent,
To adore with pagan rites the power armipotent:
Then prostrate, low before his altar lay,
And raised his manly voice, and thus began to pray: 295
"Strong God of Arms, whose iron sceptre sways
The freezing North, and Hyperborean seas,
And Scythian colds, and Thracia's wintry coast,
Where stand thy steeds, and thou art honoured most:
There most, but everywhere thy power is known,   300
The fortune of the fight is all thy own:
Terror is thine, and wild amazement, flung
From out thy chariot, withers even the strong;
And disarray and shameful rout ensue,
And force is added to the fainting crew.   305
Acknowledged as thou art, accept my prayer!
If aught I have achieved deserve thy care,
If to my utmost power with sword and shield
I dared the death, unknowing how to yield,
And falling in my rank, still kept the field;   310

Then let my arms prevail, by thee sustained,
That Emily by conquest may be gained.
Have pity on my pains; nor those unknown
To Mars, which, when a lover, were his own.
Venus, the public care of all above,   315
Thy stubborn heart has softened into love:
By those dear pleasures, aid my arms in fight,
And make me conquer in my patron's right:
For I am young, a novice in the trade,
The fool of love, unpractised to persuade,   320
And want the soothing arts that catch the fair,
But, caught myself, lie struggling in the snare;
And she I love or laughs at all my pain,
Or knows her worth too well, and pays me with disdain.
For sure I am, unless I win in arms,   325
To stand excluded from Emilia's charms:
Nor can my strength avail, unless, by thee
Endued with force, I gain the victory;
Then for the fire which warmed thy generous heart,
Pity thy subject's pains and equal smart.   330
So be the morrow's sweat and labour mine,
The palm and honour of the conquest thine:
Then shall the war, and stern debate, and strife
Immortal be the business of my life;
And in thy fane, the dusty spoils among,   335
High on the burnished roof, my banner shall be hung,
Ranked with my champions' bucklers; and below,
With arms reversed, the achievements of my foe;
And while these limbs the vital spirit feeds,
While day to night, and night to day succeeds,   340
Thy smoking altar shall be fat with food
Of incense and the grateful steam of blood;
Burnt-offerings morn and evening shall be thine,
And fires eternal in thy temple shine.
This bush of yellow beard, this length of hair,   345

Which from my birth inviolate I bear,
Guiltless of steel, and from the razor free,
Shall fall, a plenteous crop, reserved for thee.
So may my arms with victory be blest,
I ask no more; let Fate dispose the rest."   350
    The champion ceased; there followed in the close
A hollow groan; a murmuring wind arose;
The rings of iron, that on the doors were hung,
Sent out a jarring sound, and harshly rung:
The bolted gates flew open at the blast,   355
The storm rushed in, and Arcite stood aghast:
The flames were blown aside, yet shone they bright,
Fanned by the wind, and gave a ruffled light.
    Then from the ground a scent began to rise,
Sweet smelling as accepted sacrifice: 360
This omen pleased, and, as the flames aspire,
With odorous incense Arcite heaps the fire:
Nor wanted hymns to Mars or heathen charms:
At length the nodding statue clashed his arms,
And with a sullen sound and feeble cry,   365
Half sunk and half pronounced the word of Victory.
For this, with soul devout, he thanked the God,
And, of success secure, returned to his abode.
    These vows, thus granted, raised a strife above
Betwixt the God of War and Queen of Love.   370
She, granting first, had right of time to plead;
But he had granted too, nor would recede.
Jove was for Venus; but he feared his wife,
And seemed unwilling to decide the strife;
Till Saturn from his leaden throne arose,   375
And found a way the difference to compose:
Though sparing of his grace, to mischief bent,
He seldom does a good with good intent.
Wayward, but wise; by long experience taught,
To please both parties, for ill ends, he sought;   380

For this advantage age from youth has won,
As not to be outridden, though outrun.
By fortune he was now to Venus trined,
And with stern Mars in Capricorn was joined:
Of him disposing in his own abode,   385
He soothed the Goddess, while he gulled the God:
"Cease, daughter, to complain; and stint the strife;
Thy Palamon shall have his promised wife:
And Mars, the lord of conquest, in the fight
With palm and laurel shall adorn his knight.   390
Wide is my course, nor turn I to my place
Till length of time, and move with tardy pace.
Man feels me, when I press the ethereal plains;
My hand is heavy, and the wound remains.
Mine is the shipwreck in a watery sign;   395
And in an earthy, the dark dungeon mine.
Cold shivering agues, melancholy care,
And bitter blasting winds, and poisoned air,
Are mine, and wilful death, resulting from despair.
The throttling quinsy 'tis my star appoints,   400
And rheumatisms I send to rack the joints:
When churls rebel against their native prince,
I arm their hands, and furnish the pretence;
And housing in the lion's hateful sign,
Bought senates and deserting troops are mine.   405
Mine is the privy poisoning; I command
Unkindly seasons and ungrateful land.
By me kings' palaces are pushed to ground,
And miners crushed beneath their mines are found.
'Twas I slew Samson, when the pillared hall   410
Fell down, and crushed the many with the fall.
My looking is the sire of pestilence,
That sweeps at once the people and the prince.
Now weep no more, but trust thy grandsire's art;
Mars shall be pleased, and thou perform thy part.   415

'Tis ill, though different your complexions are,
The family of Heaven for men should war."
The expedient pleased, where neither lost his right;
Mars had the day, and Venus had the night.
The management they left to Chronos' care.   420
Now turn we to the effect, and sing the war.

   In Athens, all was pleasure, mirth, and play,
All proper to the spring, and sprightly May:
Which every soul inspired with such delight,
'Twas justing all the day, and love at night.   425
Heaven smiled, and gladded was the heart of man;
And Venus had the world, as when it first began.
At length in sleep their bodies they compose,
And dreamt the future fight, and early rose.

   Now scarce the dawning day began to spring,   430
As at a signal given, the streets with clamours ring:
At once the crowd arose; confused and high,
Even from the heaven was heard a shouting cry,
For Mars was early up, and roused the sky.
The gods came downward to behold the wars,   435
Sharpening their sights, and leaning from their stars.
The neighing of the generous horse was heard,
For battle by the busy groom prepared:
Rustling of harness, rattling of the shield,
Clattering of armour, furbished for the field.   440
Crowds to the castle mounted up the street,
Battering the pavement with their coursers' feet:
The greedy sight might there devour the gold
Of glittering arms, too dazzling to behold:
And polished steel that cast the view aside,   445
And crested morions, with their plumy pride.
Knights, with a long retinue of their squires,
In gaudy liveries march, and quaint attires.
One laced the helm, another held the lance;
A third the shining buckler did advance.   450

The courser pawed the ground with restless feet,
And snorting foamed, and champed the golden bit.
The smiths and armourers on palfreys ride,
Files in their hands, and hammers at their side,
And nails for loosened spears and thongs for shields provide.
The yeomen guard the streets, in seemly bands;   456
And clowns come crowding on, with cudgels in their hands.
    The trumpets, next the gate, in order placed,
Attend the sign to sound the martial blast:
The palace-yard is filled with floating tides,   460
And the last comers bear the former to the sides.
The throng is in the midst; the common crew
Shut out, the hall admits the better few.
In knots they stand, or in a rank they walk,
Serious in aspect, earnest in their talk;   465
Factious, and favouring this or t'other side,
As their strong fancies and weak reason guide;
Their wagers back their wishes; numbers hold
With the fair freckled king, and beard of gold:
So vigorous are his eyes, such rays they cast,   470
So prominent his eagle's beak is placed.
But most their looks on the black monarch bend;
His rising muscles and his brawn commend;
His double-biting axe, and beamy spear,
Each asking a gigantic force to rear.   475
All spoke as partial favour moved the mind;
And, safe themselves, at others' cost divined.
    Waked by the cries, the Athenian chief arose,
The knightly forms of combat to dispose;
And passing through the obsequious guards, he sate   480
Conspicuous on a throne, sublime in state;
There, for the two contending knights he sent;
Armed cap-a-pe, with reverence low they bent;
He smiled on both, and with superior look
Alike their offered adoration took.   485

The people press on every side to see
Their awful prince, and hear his high decree.
Then signing to the heralds with his hand,
They gave his orders from their lofty stand.
Silence is thrice enjoined; then thus aloud   490
The king-at-arms bespeaks the knights and listening crowd:
  "Our sovereign lord has pondered in his mind
The means to spare the blood of gentle kind;
And of his grace and inborn clemency
He modifies his first severe decree,   495
The keener edge of battle to rebate,
The troops for honour fighting, not for hate.
He wills not death should terminate their strife,
And wounds, if wounds ensue, be short of life;
But issues, ere the fight, his dread command,   500
That slings afar, and poniards hand to hand,
Be banished from the field; that none shall dare
With shortened sword to stab in closer war;
But in fair combat fight with manly strength,
Nor push with biting point, but strike at length.   505
The turney is allowed but one career
Of the tough ash, with the sharp-grinded spear;
But knights unhorsed may rise from off the plain,
And fight on foot their honour to regain;
Nor, if at mischief taken, on the ground   510
Be slain, but prisoners to the pillar bound,
At either barrier placed; nor (captives made)
Be freed, or armed anew the fight invade.
The chief of either side, bereft of life
Or yielded to his foe, concludes the strife.   515
Thus dooms the lord: now, valiant knights and young,
Fight each his fill, with swords and maces long."
  The herald ends; the vaulted firmament
With loud acclaims and vast applause is rent:
Heaven guard a prince so gracious and so good,   520

So just, and yet so provident of blood!
This was the general cry.   The trumpets sound,
And warlike symphony is heard around.
The marching troops through Athens take their way,
The great earl-marshal orders their array.   525
The fair from high the passing pomp behold;
A rain of flowers is from the windows rolled.
The casements are with golden tissue spread,
And horses' hoofs, for earth, on silken tapestry tread.
The king goes midmost, and the rivals ride   530
In equal rank, and close his either side.
Next after these there rode the royal wife,
With Emily, the cause and the reward of strife.
The following cavalcade, by three and three,
Proceed by titles marshalled in degree.   535
Thus through the southern gate they take their way,
And at the list arrived ere prime of day.
There, parting from the king, the chiefs divide,
And wheeling east and west, before their many ride.
The Athenian monarch mounts his throne on high,   540
And after him the queen and Emily:
Next these, the kindred of the crown are graced
With nearer seats, and lords by ladies placed.
Scarce were they seated, when with clamours loud
In rushed at once a rude promiscuous crowd: 545
The guards, and then each other, overbear,
And in a moment throng the spacious theatre.
Now changed the jarring noise to whispers low,
As winds, forsaking seas, more softly blow,
When at the western gate, on which the car   550
Is placed aloft that bears the God of War,
Proud Arcite, entering armed before his train,
Stops at the barrier, and divides the plain.
Red was his banner, and displayed abroad
The bloody colours of his patron god.   555

At that self moment enters Palamon
The gate of Venus, and the rising Sun;
Waved by the wanton winds, his banner flies,
All maiden white, and shares the people's eyes.
From east to west, look all the world around,   560
Two troops so matched were never to be found;
Such bodies built for strength, of equal age,
In stature sized; so proud an equipage:
The nicest eye could no distinction make,
Where lay the advantage, or what side to take.   565
    Thus ranged, the herald for the last proclaims
A silence, while they answered to their names:
For so the king decreed, to shun with care
The fraud of musters false, the common bane of war.
The tale was just, and then the gates were closed;   570
And chief to chief, and troop to troop opposed.
The heralds last retired, and loudly cried:
" The fortune of the field be fairly tried ! "
    At this the challenger, with fierce defy,
His trumpet sounds; the challenged makes reply;   575
With clangour rings the field, resounds the vaulted sky;
Their vizors closed, their lances in the rest,
Or at the helmet pointed, or the crest,
They vanish from the barrier, speed the race,
And spurring see decrease the middle space.   580
A cloud of smoke envelopes either host,
And all at once the combatants are lost:
Darkling they join adverse, and shock unseen,
Coursers with coursers justling, men with men:
As labouring in eclipse, a while they stay,   585
Till the next blast of wind restores the day.
They look anew: the beauteous form of fight
Is changed, and war appears a grisly sight.
Two troops in fair array one moment showed,
The next, a field with fallen bodies strewed: 590

Not half the number in their seats are found;
But men and steeds lie grovelling on the ground.
The points of spears are stuck within the shield,
The steeds without their riders scour the field.
The knights, unhorsed, on foot renew the fight;   595
The glittering falchions cast a gleaming light;
Hauberks and helms are hewed with many a wound;
Out spins the streaming blood, and dyes the ground.
The mighty maces with such haste descend,
They break the bones, and make the solid armour bend. 600
This thrusts amid the throng with furious force;
Down goes, at once, the horseman and the horse:
That courser stumbles on the fallen steed,
And, floundering, throws the rider o'er his head.
One rolls along, a football to his foes;   605
One with a broken truncheon deals his blows.
This halting, this disabled with his wound,
In triumph led, is to the pillar bound,
Where by the king's award he must abide;
There goes a captive led on t'other side.   610
By fits they cease, and leaning on the lance,
Take breath a while, and to new fight advance.
    Full oft the rivals met, and neither spared
His utmost force, and each forgot to ward:
The head of this was to the saddle bent,   615
That other backward to the crupper sent:
Both were by turns unhorsed; the jealous blows
Fall thick and heavy, when on foot they close.
So deep their falchions bite, that every stroke
Pierced to the quick; and equal wounds they gave and took.
Borne far asunder by the tides of men,   621
Like adamant and steel they met again.
    So when a tiger sucks the bullock's blood,
A famished lion, issuing from the wood,
Roars lordly fierce, and challenges the food.   625

Each claims possession, neither will obey,
But both their paws are fastened on the prey;
They bite, they tear; and while in vain they strive,
The swains come armed between, and both to distance drive.

At length, as fate foredoomed, and all things tend   630
By course of time to their appointed end;
So when the sun to west was far declined,
And both afresh in mortal battle joined,
The strong Emetrius came in Arcite's aid,
And Palamon with odds was overlaid: 635
For, turning short, he struck with all his might
Full on the helmet of the unwary knight.
Deep was the wound; he staggered with the blow,
And turned him to his unexpected foe;
Whom with such force he struck, he felled him down,   640
And cleft the circle of his golden crown.
But Arcite's men, who now prevailed in fight,
Twice ten at once surround the single knight:
O'erpowered at length, they force him to the ground,
Unyielded as he was, and to the pillar bound;   645
And king Lycurgus, while he fought in vain
His friend to free, was tumbled on the plain.

Who now laments but Palamon, compelled
No more to try the fortune of the field,
And, worse than death, to view with hateful eyes   650
His rival's conquest, and renounce the prize!
The royal judge on his tribunal placed,
Who had beheld the fight from first to last,
Bade cease the war; pronouncing from on high,
Arcite of Thebes had won the beauteous Emily.   655
The sound of trumpets to the voice replied,
And round the royal lists the heralds cried:
"Arcite of Thebes has won the beauteous bride!"
The people rend the skies with vast applause;
All own the chief, when Fortune owns the cause.   660

Arcite is owned even by the gods above,
And conquering Mars insults the Queen of Love.
So laughed he when the rightful Titan failed,
And Jove's usurping arms in heaven prevailed.
Laughed all the powers who favour tyranny,   665
And all the standing army of the sky.
But Venus with dejected eyes appears,
And, weeping, on the lists distilled her tears;
Her will refused, which grieves a woman most,
And, in her champion foiled, the cause of Love is lost.   670
Till Saturn said: "Fair daughter, now be still:
The blustering fool has satisfied his will;
His boon is given; his knight has gained the day,
But lost the prize; the arrears are yet to pay.
Thy hour is come, and mine the care shall be   675
To please thy knight, and set thy promise free."
  Now while the heralds run the lists around,
And Arcite! Arcite! heaven and earth resound;
A miracle (nor less it could be called)
Their joy with unexpected sorrow palled.   680
The victor knight had laid his helm aside,
Part for his ease, the greater part for pride;
Bareheaded, popularly low he bowed,
And paid the salutations of the crowd.
Then spurring at full speed, ran endlong on   685
Where Theseus sat on his imperial throne;
Furious he drove, and upward cast his eye,
Where, next the Queen, was placed his Emily;
Then passing, to the saddle-bow he bent;
A sweet regard the gracious virgin lent   690
(For women, to the brave an easy prey,
Still follow Fortune where she leads the way);
Just then from earth sprung out a flashing fire,
By Pluto sent, at Saturn's bad desire:
The startling steed was seized with sudden fright,   695

And, bounding, o'er the pummel cast the knight;
Forward he flew, and pitching on his head,
He quivered with his feet, and lay for dead.
Black was his countenance in a little space,
For all the blood was gathered in his face.   700
Help was at hand: they reared him from the ground,
And from his cumbrous arms his limbs unbound;
Then lanced a vein, and watched returning breath;
It came, but clogged with symptoms of his death.
The saddle-bow the noble parts had pressed,   705
All bruised and mortified his manly breast.
Him still entranced, and in a litter laid,
They bore from field, and to his bed conveyed.
At length he waked; and, with a feeble cry,
The word he first pronounced was Emily.   710
    Meantime the king, though inwardly he mourned,
In pomp triumphant to the town returned,
Attended by the chiefs who fought the field
(Now friendly mixed, and in one troop compelled),
Composed his looks to counterfeited cheer,   715
And bade them not for Arcite's life to fear.
But that which gladded all the warrior train,
Though most were sorely wounded, none were slain.
The surgeons soon despoiled them of their arms,
And some with salves they cure, and some with charms;   720
Foment the bruises, and the pains assuage,
And heal their inward hurts with sovereign draughts of sage.
The king in person visits all around,
Comforts the sick, congratulates the sound;
Honours the princely chiefs, rewards the rest,   725
And holds for thrice three days a royal feast.
None was disgraced; for falling is no shame,
And cowardice alone is loss of fame.
The venturous knight is from the saddle thrown,
But 'tis the fault of fortune, not his own;   730

If crowds and palms the conquering side adorn,
The victor under better stars was born:
The brave man seeks not popular applause,
Nor, overpowered with arms, deserts his cause;
Unshamed, though foiled, he does the best he can: 735
Force is of brutes, but honour is of man.
   Thus Theseus smiled on all with equal grace,
And each was set according to his place;
With ease were reconciled the differing parts,
For envy never dwells in noble hearts.   740
At length they took their leave, the time expired,
Well pleased, and to their several homes retired.
   Meanwhile, the health of Arcite still impairs;
From bad proceeds to worse, and mocks the leeches' cares:
Swollen is his breast; his inward pains increase;   745
All means are used, and all without success.
The clotted blood lies heavy on his heart,
Corrupts, and there remains in spite of art;
Nor breathing veins nor cupping will prevail;
All outward remedies and inward fail.   750
The mould of nature's fabric is destroyed,
Her vessels discomposed, her virtue void:
The bellows of his lungs begins to swell;
All out of frame is every secret cell,
Nor can the good receive, nor bad expel.   755
Those breathing organs, thus within oppressed,
With venom soon distend the sinews of his breast.
Nought profits him to save abandoned life,
Nor vomit's upward aid, nor downward laxative.
The midmost region battered and destroyed,   760
When nature cannot work, the effect of art is void:
For physic can but mend our crazy state,
Patch an old building, not a new create.
Arcite is doomed to die in all his pride,
Must leave his youth, and yield his beauteous bride,   765

Gained hardly, against right, and unenjoyed.
When 'twas declared all hope of life was past,
Conscience, that of all physic works the last,
Caused him to send for Emily in haste.
With her, at his desire, came Palamon;   770
Then, on his pillow raised, he thus begun:
"No language can express the smallest part
Of what I feel, and suffer in my heart,
For you, whom best I love and value most,
But to your service I bequeath my ghost;   775
Which, from this mortal body when untied,
Unseen, unheard, shall hover at your side;
Nor fright you waking, nor your sleep offend,
But wait officious, and your steps attend.
How I have loved, — excuse my faltering tongue,   780
My spirit's feeble, and my pains are strong :
This I may say, I only grieve to die,
Because I lose my charming Emily.
To die, when Heaven had put you in my power!
Fate could not choose a more malicious hour.   785
What greater curse could envious Fortune give,
Than just to die when I began to live!
Vain men! how vanishing a bliss we crave,
Now warm in love, now withering in the grave!
Never, oh never more to see the sun!   790
Still dark, in a damp vault, and still alone!
This fate is common; but I lose my breath
Near bliss, and yet not blessed, before my death.
Farewell! but take me dying in your arms;
'Tis all I can enjoy of all your charms: 795
This hand I cannot but in death resign;
Ah, could I live! but while I live 'tis mine.
I feel my end approach, and thus embraced
Am pleased to die; but hear me speak my last:
Ah, my sweet foe! for you, and you alone,   800

I broke my faith with injured Palamon.
But love the sense of right and wrong confounds;
Strong love and proud ambition have no bounds.
And much I doubt, should Heaven my life prolong,
I should return to justify my wrong;   805
For, while my former flames remain within,
Repentance is but want of power to sin.
With mortal hatred I pursued his life,
Nor he, nor you, were guilty of the strife;
Nor I, but as I loved; yet all combined,   810
Your beauty, and my impotence of mind,
And his concurrent flame that blew my fire;
For still our kindred souls had one desire.
He had a moment's right in point of time;
Had I seen first, then his had been the crime.   815
Fate made it mine, and justified his right;
Nor holds this earth a more deserving knight
For virtue, valour, and for noble blood,
Truth, honour, all that is comprised in good;
So help me Heaven, in all the world is none   820
So worthy to be loved as Palamon.
He loves you too, with such a holy fire,
As will not, cannot, but with life expire:
Our vowed affections both have often tried,
Nor any love but yours could ours divide.   825
Then, by my love's inviolable band,
By my long suffering and my short command,
If e'er you plight your vows when I am gone,
Have pity on the faithful Palamon."
     This was his last; for Death came on amain,   830
And exercised below his iron reign;
Then upward to the seat of life he goes;
Sense fled before him, what he touched he froze:
Yet could he not his closing eyes withdraw,
Though less and less of Emily he saw;   835

So, speechless, for a little space he lay;
Then grasped the hand he held, and sighed his soul away.
  But whither went his soul, let such relate
Who search the secrets of the future state:
Divines can say but what themselves believe;   840
Strong proofs they have, but not demonstrative;
For, were all plain, then all sides must agree,
And faith itself be lost in certainty.
To live uprightly, then, is sure the best;
To save ourselves, and not to damn the rest.   845
The soul of Arcite went where heathens go,
Who better live than we, though less they know.
  In Palamon a manly grief appears;
Silent he wept, ashamed to show his tears.
Emilia shrieked but once; and then, oppressed   850
With sorrow, sunk upon her lover's breast:
Till Theseus in his arms conveyed with care,
Far from so sad a sight, the swooning fair.
'Twere loss of time her sorrow to relate;
Ill bears the sex a youthful lover's fate,   855
When just approaching to the nuptial state:
But, like a low-hung cloud, it rains so fast,
That all at once it falls, and cannot last.
The face of things is changed, and Athens now.
That laughed so late, becomes the scene of woe: 860
Matrons and maids, both sexes, every state,
With tears lament the knight's untimely fate.
Not greater grief in falling Troy was seen
For Hector's death; but Hector was not then.
Old men with dust deformed their hoary hair;   865
The women beat their breasts, their cheeks they tear.
" Why wouldst thou go," with one consent they cry,
" When thou hadst gold enough, and Emily ? "
Theseus himself, who should have cheered the grief
Of others, wanted now the same relief: 870

Old Ægeus only could revive his son,
Who various changes of the world had known,
And strange vicissitudes of human fate,
Still altering, never in a steady state:
Good after ill and, after pain, delight,   875
Alternate, like the scenes of day and night.
Since every man who lives is born to die,
And none can boast sincere felicity,
With equal mind, what happens, let us bear,
Nor joy, nor grieve too much, for things beyond our care.
Like pilgrims to the appointed place we tend;   881
The world's an inn, and death the journey's end.
Even kings but play, and when their part is done,
Some other, worse or better, mount the throne.
With words like these the crowd was satisfied;   885
And so they would have been, had Theseus died.
    But he, their king, was labouring in his mind
A fitting place for funeral pomps to find,
Which were in honour of the dead designed.
And, after long debate, at last he found   890
(As Love itself had marked the spot of ground)
That grove for ever green, that conscious laund,
Where he with Palamon fought hand to hand;
That, where he fed his amorous desires
With soft complaints, and felt his hottest fires,   895
There other flames might waste his earthly part,
And burn his limbs, where love had burned his heart.
    This once resolved, the peasants were enjoined
Sere wood, and firs, and doddered oaks to find.
With sounding axes to the grove they go,   900
Fell, split, and lay the fuel in a row,
Vulcanian food: a bier is next prepared,
On which the lifeless body should be reared,
Covered with cloth of gold; on which was laid
The corpse of Arcite, in like robes arrayed.   905

White gloves were on his hands, and on his head
A wreath of laurel, mixed with myrtle, spread.
A sword, keen-edged, within his right he held,
The warlike emblem of the conquered field.
Bare was his manly visage on the bier;   910
Menaced his countenance, even in death severe.
Then to the palace-hall they bore the knight,
To lie in solemn state, a public sight:
Groans, cries, and howlings fill the crowded place,
And unaffected sorrow sat on every face.   915
Sad Palamon above the rest appears,
In sable garments, dewed with gushing tears;
His auburn locks on either shoulder flowed,
Which to the funeral of his friend he vowed;
But Emily, as chief, was next his side,   920
A virgin-widow, and a mourning bride.
And, that the princely obsequies might be
Performed according to his high degree,
The steed that bore him living to the fight
Was trapped with polished steel, all shining bright,   925
And covered with the achievements of the knight.
The riders rode abreast, and one his shield,
His lance of cornel-wood another held;
The third his bow, and, glorious to behold,
The costly quiver, all of burnished gold.   930
The noblest of the Grecians next appear,
And weeping, on their shoulders bore the bier;
With sober pace they marched, and often stayed,
And through the master-street the corpse conveyed.
The houses to their tops with black were spread,   935
And even the pavements were with mourning hid.
The right side of the pall old Ægeus kept,
And on the left the royal Theseus wept;
Each bore a golden bowl, of work divine,
With honey filled, and milk, and mixed with ruddy wine.

ₒu Palamon, the kinsman of the slain,   941
A   after him appeared the illustrious train.
To grace the pomp came Emily the bright,
With covered fire, the funeral pile to light.
With high devotion was the service made,   945
And all the rites of pagan honour paid:
So lofty was the pile, a Parthian bow,
With vigour drawn, must send the shaft below.
The bottom was full twenty fathom broad,
With crackling straw beneath in due proportion strewed.
The fabric seemed a wood of rising green,   951
With sulphur and bitumen cast between,
To feed the flames; the trees were unctuous fir,
And mountain-ash, the mother of the spear;
The mourner-yew and builder-oak were there,   955
The beech, the swimming alder, and the plane,
Hard box and linden of a softer grain,
And laurels, which the gods for conquering chiefs ordain.
How they were ranked shall rest untold by me,
With nameless nymphs that lived in every tree;   960
Nor how the Dryads and the woodland train,
Disherited, ran howling o'er the plain;
Nor how the birds to foreign seats repaired,
Or beasts that bolted out and saw the forest bared:
Nor how the ground, now cleared, with ghastly fright   965
Beheld the sudden sun, a stranger to the light.
    The straw, as first I said, was laid below;
Of chips and sere wood was the second row;
The third of greens, and timber newly felled;
The fourth high stage the fragrant odours held,   970
And pearls, and precious stones, in rich array;
In midst of which, embalmed, the body lay.
The service sung, the maid, with mourning eyes,
The stubble fired; the smouldering flames arise:
This office done, she sunk upon the ground;   975

But what she spoke, recovered from her swound,
I want the wit in moving words to dress;
But by themselves the tender sex may guess.
While the devouring fire was burning fast,
Rich jewels in the flame the wealthy cast;   980
And some their shields, and some their lances threw,
And gave the warrior's ghost a warrior's due.
Full bowls of wine, of honey, milk, and blood
Were poured upon the pile of burning wood,
And hissing flames receive, and, hungry, lick the food.   985
Then thrice the mounted squadrons ride around
The fire, and Arcite's name they thrice resound:
" Hail and farewell ! " they shouted thrice amain,
Thrice facing to the left, and thrice they turned again:
Still, as they turned, they beat their clattering shields;   990
The women mix their cries, and clamour fills the fields.
The warlike wakes continued all the night,
And funeral games were played at new returning light:
Who naked wrestled best, besmeared with oil,
Or who with gauntlets gave or took the foil,   995
I will not tell you, nor would you attend;
But briefly haste to my long story's end.
    I pass the rest; the year was fully mourned,
And Palamon long since to Thebes returned:
When, by the Grecians' general consent,   1000
At Athens Theseus held his parliament;
Among the laws that passed, it was decreed,
That conquered Thebes from bondage should be freed:
Reserving homage to the Athenian throne,
To which the sovereign summoned Palamon.   1005
Unknowing of the cause, he took his way,
Mournful in mind, and still in black array.
    The monarch mounts the throne, and, placed on high,
Commands into the court the beauteous Emily.
So called, she came; the senate rose, and paid   1010

Becoming reverence to the royal maid.
And first, soft whispers through the assembly went;
With silent wonder then they watched the event;
All hushed, the king arose with awful grace;
Deep thought was in his breast, and counsel in his face: 1015
At length he sighed, and, having first prepared
The attentive audience, thus his will declared:
   "The cause and spring of motion, from above,
Hung down on earth the golden chain of Love;
Great was the effect, and high was his intent,   1020
When peace among the jarring seeds he sent;
Fire, flood, and earth, and air by this were bound,
And Love, the common link, the new creation crowned.
The chain still holds; for, though the forms decay,
Eternal matter never wears away: 1025
The same first mover certain bounds has placed,
How long those perishable forms shall last;
Nor can they last beyond the time assigned
By that all-seeing and all-making Mind:
Shorten their hours they may, for will is free,   1030
But never pass the appointed destiny.
So men oppressed, when weary of their breath,
Throw off the burden, and suborn their death.
Then, since those forms begin, and have their end,
On some unaltered cause they sure depend: 1035
Parts of the whole are we, but God the whole,
Who gives us life, and animating soul.
For nature cannot from a part derive
That being which the whole can only give:
He perfect, stable; but imperfect we,   1040
Subject to change, and different in degree;
Plants, beasts, and man; and, as our organs are,
We more or less of his perfection share.
But, by a long descent, the ethereal fire
Corrupts; and forms, the mortal part, expire.   1045

As he withdraws his virtue, so they pass,
And the same matter makes another mass.
This law the omniscient Power was pleased to give,
That every kind should by succession live;
That individuals die, his will ordains;   1050
The propagated species still remains.
The monarch oak, the patriarch of the trees,
Shoots rising up, and spreads by slow degrees;
Three centuries he grows, and three he stays,
Supreme in state, and in three more decays: 1055
So wears the paving pebble in the street,
And towns and towers their fatal periods meet:
So rivers, rapid once, now naked lie,
Forsaken of their springs, and leave their channels dry.
So man, at first a drop, dilates with heat,   1060
Then, formed, the little heart begins to beat;
Secret he feeds, unknowing, in the cell;
At length, for hatching ripe, he breaks the shell,
And struggles into breath, and cries for aid;
Then helpless in his mother's lap is laid.   1065
He creeps, he walks, and, issuing into man,
Grudges their life from whence his own began;
Retchless of laws, affects to rule alone,
Anxious to reign, and restless on the throne;
First vegetive, then feels, and reasons last;   1070
Rich of three souls, and lives all three to waste.
Some thus; but thousands more in flower of age,
For few arrive to run the latter stage.
Sunk in the first, in battle some are slain,
And others whelmed beneath the stormy main.   1075
What makes all this but Jupiter the king,
At whose command we perish, and we spring?
Then 'tis our best, since thus ordained to die,
To make a virtue of necessity;
Take what he gives, since to rebel is vain;   1080

The bad grows better, which we will sustain;
And could we choose the time, and choose aright,
'Tis best to die, our honour at the height.
When we have done our ancestors no shame,
But served our friends, and well secured our fame;   1085
Then should we wish our happy life to close,
And leave no more for fortune to dispose;
So should we make our death a glad relief
From future shame, from sickness, and from grief;
Enjoying while we live the present hour,   1090
And dying in our excellence and flower.
Then round our death-bed every friend should run,
And joy us of our conquest early won;
While the malicious world, with envious tears,
Should grudge our happy end, and wish it theirs.   1095
Since then our Arcite is with honour dead,
Why should we mourn, that he so soon is freed,
Or call untimely, what the gods decreed ?
With grief as just, a friend may be deplored,
From a foul prison to free air restored.   1100
Ought he to thank his kinsman or his wife,
Could tears recall him into wretched life ?
Their sorrow hurts themselves; on him is lost,
And, worse than both, offends his happy ghost.
What then remains, but after past annoy   1105
To take the good vicissitude of joy;
To thank the gracious gods for what they give,
Possess our souls, and, while we live, to live ?
Ordain we then two sorrows to combine,
And in one point the extremes of grief to join;   1110
That thence resulting joy may be renewed,
As jarring notes in harmony conclude.
Then I propose that Palamon shall be
In marriage joined with beauteous Emily;
For which already I have gained the assent   1115

Of my free people in full parliament.
Long love to her has borne the faithful knight,
And well deserved, had Fortune done him right:
'Tis time to mend her fault, since Emily,
By Arcite's death, from former vows is free;   1120
If you, fair sister, ratify the accord,
And take him for your husband and your lord,
'Tis no dishonour to confer your grace
On one descended from a. royal race;
And were he less, yet years of service past   1125
From grateful souls exact reward at last.
Pity is heaven's and yours, nor can she find
A throne so soft as in a woman's mind."
He said; she blushed; and as o'erawed by might,
Seemed to give Theseus what she gave the knight.   1130
Then, turning to the Theban, thus he said:
" Small arguments are needful to persuade
Your temper to comply with my command: "
And speaking thus, he gave Emilia's hand.
Smiled Venus, to behold her own true knight   1135
Obtain the conquest, though he lost the fight.
All of a tenor was their after-life,
No day discoloured with domestic strife;
No jealousy, but mutual truth believed,
Secure repose, and kindness undeceived.   1140
Thus Heaven, beyond the compass of his thought,
Sent him the blessing he so dearly bought.
So may the Queen of Love long duty bless,
And all true lovers find the same success!

GLOSSARY

OF

OBSOLETE WORDS AND PECULIAR PHRASES.

—•◦•—

Book I.   Line 29.   "Forborne."   Omitted.
"Accidents."   Events.
Line 36.   "Mended with a new."   Improved by a new story.
Line 41.   "Quire."   A group.   Not necessarily singers.
Line 56.   "Sounded."   Swooned.
Line 92.   "Kind."   Kindred.
Line 98.   "Crew."   Crowd.
Line 117.   "Generous."   Abundant and approving.
Line 132.   "Howling."   Chaucerian for crying, lamenting.
Line 178.   "Gentle."   High-born.
Line 232.   "Inevitable."   Not to be escaped.
Line 240.   "Cheer."   Pleasant looks.
Line 262.   "Confess."   Show.
Line 306.   "Thy bad pretence."   Object wickedly sought.
Line 332.   "Vindicate."   Avenge.
Line 346.   "Justle."   Jostle.   Contend.
Line 382.   "Finds his dear purchase."   Finds freedom dear.
Line 427.   "Guilty of their vows."   A doubtful phrase; perhaps
having broken their vows.
Line 441.   "Starve."   Perish, not necessarily by hunger.
Line 445.   "Outrageous."   Beyond measure.
Line 457.   "Vindicate."   Avenge.
Line 492.   "At unaware."   Unawares.
Line 493.   "Forelays."   Waylays.
Line 495.   "Thrids."   Threads, or slides through.
Line 531.   "Boxen."   Of the box tree.
Line 540.   "Trim."   Garb, dress.
Line 542.   "Rage."   Insanity.
Line 593.   "Condition."   Manners.
Line 602.   "Entertained."   Paid liberally.

Book II.   Line 12. " Which forms in causes."   Originates.
Line 34. " Style."   Stylus, Latin for pen.
Line 65. " Secret."   In secret, or in hiding.
Line 83. " Cheer."   Cheerful looks.
Line 150. " In thy despite."   In spite of thee.
Line 165. " To pawn."   Pledged his faith.
Line 182. " Hopes."   Expects.
Line 188. " Generous."   Abundant.
Line 191. " None."   Neither, or no one.
Line 196. " Foin."   Push in fencing, thrust.
Line 202. " Fell."   Savage.
           " Fared."   Original meaning, to travel ; here, advanced.
Line 235. " Laund."   A lawn.
Line 237. " Forth-right."   Straightway.
Line 245. " Strook."   Struck.
Line 318. " Mastership."   Masterpiece.
Line 340. " Looked under."   Looked down.
Line 361. " Their own despite."   Here, to their hurt.
Line 369. " Their monarch's pay."   Love's reward.
Line 387. " On this accord."   With this understanding.
Line 410. " In royal lists."   " In," in place of " into."
Line 414. " Bars."   Barriers, bounds.
Line 415. " Recreant."   Yielding, surrendering.
Line 462. " The gate opposed."   The opposite gate.
Line 467. " Oratories."   Places of worship, chapels.
Line 478. " Assurance."   Of assured love.
Line 483. " Sigils."   Seals, with planetary signs.
Line 489. " Cuckow."   A bird, emblematic of misleading.
Line 519. " Turtles."   Turtle-doves.
           " Buxom air."   Pliant or wanton.
Line 524. " Dome."   House, palace.
Line 534. " Scurf."   Scales.
Line 536. " Knares."   Stubby protuberances.
Line 544. " On a bent."   Slope of a hill.
Line 545. " Armipotent."   Powerful in arms.
Line 549. " Blind."   No apertures for looking out.
Line 577. " Clottered."   Clotted.
Line 583. " Complaint on theft."   Because of theft.
Line 590. " Overlaid."   Killed by lying upon it.
Line 600. " Scarlet conquest."   Bloody conqueror.
Line 604. " Mars his ides."   The Ides of March.

Line 614. "Geomantic." Astrological.
Line 623. "Manifest of shame." Openly exposed.
Line 630. "Mistaken," for a stag.
Line 633. "Fane." Temple.
Line 649. "Wexing." Waxing.
Line 658. "Mend." Exceed, surpass.

Book III. Line 24. " Their arms were several." Different.
Line 31. "Pruce." Prussia.
Line 35. "Jambeux." Greaves, to defend the legs.
Line 57. "Pards." Leopards.
Line 68. "Orient." Shining, brilliant.
Line 89. "Reclaimed." Tamed.
Line 96. "The increase of arms." Improvement in arms.
Line 100. "Honest god." Noble, worthy of honor.
Line 101. "The war of either side." Warriors.
Line 103. "At prime." Earlier part of the day.
Line 109. "Harbinger." Herald or messenger.
Line 123. "Flickering." Fluttering.
Line 124. "Preventing day." Getting the start of.
Line 145. "Gladder." One who makes glad.
Line 208. "Mastless oak." Barren.
Line 222. "Feathered deaths." Arrows producing death. The result used in place of the instrument.
Line 231. "Gust." Latin, *gusto*, to taste ; zest, appetite.
Line 270. "Cornel spear." Cornel tree, a species of dogwood.
Line 323. "Or laughs." "Or" for "either."
Line 338. "Achievements." Escutcheons. Armorial ensigns.
Line 351. "The close." The area inclosed.
Line 366. "Half sunk." Half smothered.
Line 383. "Trined." Put in a favorable astronomic position.
Line 387. "Stint." To cease.
Line 416. "Complexions." Dispositions.
Line 446. "Crested morions." Helmets without visors.
Line 474. "Beamy spear." Beam or handle, betokening size.
Line 483. "Cap-a-pe." Cap-a-pie. French term for completely.
Line 491. "King-at-arms." Chief of heralds.
Line 505. "Strike at length." Standing off.
Line 510. "At mischief taken." At disadvantage.
Line 516. "Dooms." Decides or gives a decree.
Line 539. "Many." The chief's retinue.

Line 556. "Self moment."   Same moment.
Line 563. "Sized."   Mated.
           "Equipage."   Equipment.
Line 583. "Darkling."   Being in the dark.
Line 597. "Hauberks."   Coats of mail.
Line 635. "Overlaid."   Oppressed.
Line 685. "Endlong on."   In a straight line.
Line 707. "Entranced."   Unconscious.
Line 721. "Foment."   Bathe with warm lotions.
Line 749. "Breathing veins."   Blood-letting from veins.
Line 779. "Officious."   To offer services.
Line 878. "Sincere."   Real, genuine, without alloy.
Line 892. "Conscious laund."   The spot or lawn, personified.
Line 899. "Doddered."   Overgrown with parasites.
Line 926. "Achievements."   See Book III. 338.
Line 934. "Master-street."   Main avenue.
Line 956. "Swimming Alder."   The tree thrives in swamps.
Line 995. "Took the foil."   Blunt sword. Possibly here, defeat.
Line 1021. "Jarring seeds."   Conflicting elements.
Line 1033. "Suborn."   To procure by indirect means.
Line 1068. "Retchless."   Reckless.

NOTES.

----◦◇◦----

"The Knight's Tale." The knight who is supposed to tell this story is the noble, among the pilgrims to Canterbury, in the latter part of the fourteenth century. He has been in the wars against the infidels; he has with him his squire, and, as might be expected, his tale is of men and women of gentle blood and of romantic love and deeds of chivalry.

The company of twenty-nine pilgrims is a motley crowd, and they beguile the way by telling stories. Hence, we have "The Knight's Tale," "The Miller's Tale," "The Clerk's," "The Merchant's," "The Nun's," "The Doctor's," "The Wife of Bath's," and others, making more than a score of tales, each of its own peculiar sort.

There is an inscription on an inn, now called "The Talbot," in Southwark: "This is the Inn where Sir Jeffrey Chaucer and the twenty-nine pilgrims lodged, in their journey to Canterbury, Anno. 1383." This inscription is evidently of a recent date, and the sign had been changed from the Tabard to the Talbot. It is possible that this was the inn which Chaucer had in mind in the twenty-first line of his "Knight's Tale."

Taine, in his "History of English Literature" (Vol. II., Book III., Ch. II.), calls attention to the difference between Chaucer and Dryden. The student would do well to read the whole chapter, remembering that Taine sometimes censures English writers undeservedly.

The student should also compare Chaucer's version of "The Knight's Tale" with Dryden's, at least in some parts of the Tale. For example, compare Chaucer's graceful style in lines 2772–2784, the speech of the dying Arcite, with Dryden's version of the same incident, Book III., 780–799. Taine says that Dryden lacks Chaucer's "astonished carelessness and graceful gossip," which the student may possibly find for himself in the older version.

Dryden's "Knight's Tale" is in three books of different lengths; Chaucer's, four books of about the same number of lines each. Dryden has one hundred and sixteen lines more than Chaucer in this tale.

90

While he omits some of Chaucer's ideas, he introduces several of his own, not always to the improvement of Chaucer's simplicity of thought. See, for example, Book II., 115 ; Book III., 20-21, 402, 665, 842-847. The student may also study Dryden's "Knight's Tale," to see if he agrees with Dr. Samuel Johnson's criticism, in his "Life of Dryden," that "the story of Palamon and Arcite (containing an action unsuitable to the times in which it was placed) is not to be highly praised." The same author speaks of Dryden's "uneven compositions," and his "faults of affectation and of negligence." Some of these criticisms the student may agree with ; but, as a whole, the Tale will be found to be a delightful one, presenting vigorously, and always with effective descriptions, the poetic and romantic side of grand pageants, heroic and courtly characters, and interesting situations.

Book I. Line 2. "Theseus." King of Athens. In legend, he killed The Minotaur, conquered Amazons and Thebans ; one of the Argonauts.

Line 7. "Scythia." Northern Europe and Asia. — "Warrior queen." Hippolyta.

Line 17. "Amazons." Caucasian race of female warriors.

Line 31. "Mine host." See previous note. The Talbot inn.

Line 76. "Capaneus." A hero, slain in the siege of Thebes.

Line 77. "Thebes." A city of Bœotia.

Line 81. "Creon." King of Thebes.

Line 109. "Argent field." On his white banner, Mars.

Line 116. "Minotaur." A monster with a bull's head. Slain in the Labyrinth of Minos by Theseus.

Line 170. "Emilia." Emily, pronounced to suit the meter throughout the Tale.

Line 186. "Aurora." Goddess of Dawn.

Line 191. "At every turn." Compare "Paradise Lost," Book IX., 425-430.

Line 199. "Philomel." Daughter of Pandion, changed into a nightingale.

Line 245. "Our horoscope." To be born with Saturn in the ascendant was a bad omen.

Line 249. "By Destiny." The ancient idea of Fate was an arbitrary law, irrespective of moral character.

Line 258. "Actæon." Grandson of Cadmus ; slain by Diana's hounds. See Smith's "Dictionary of Mythology."

Line 260. "Juno." Wife of Jupiter.

Line 261. "Cyprian queen." Venus.

Line 291. "Our holy oath." Compare the story of Damon and Pythias.

Line 209. "Traitor." Love, as the god Cupid, was supposed to have transforming power.

Line 309. "My eldership of right." Palamon saw Emily first ; Arcite claims that he loved her first, as a woman.

Line 342. "Æsop's hounds." Author of the Fables of Æsop.

Line 358. "Pirithous." A Thessalian prince ; was killed by Cerberus, guardian of Hades.

Line 421. "Of Fortune, Fate, or Providence complain ?" Compare Chaucer's lines : —

> "Alas ! why plainen [complain] men so, in commune,
> Of purveyance [Providence] of God, or of fortune."

Line 499. "And Juno's wrath." Cadmus slew the Dragon, sacred to Mars ; therefore Juno and Mars cursed all his race.

Line 515. "Beholds whate'er he would." Notice the Alexandrine meter, of six feet. The sense is, that Arcite beholds everything, except the only thing that he desires to behold.

Line 516. Chaucer asks lovers in general to decide the question which of the two, Palamon or Arcite, had the better lot.

Line 547. "Hermes." Mercury. Messenger of the gods.

Line 550. "Sleep-compelling rod." Staff of office, with wings at the top and two serpents around it.

Line 552. "Argus' head." Mercury put this hundred-eyed giant to sleep and then killed him. Compare poetic description of the *caduceus*, or wand, in Pope's "Odyssey," Book XXIV.

Line 590. "Philostratus." In "A Midsummer Night's Dream," a Philostrate is introduced as a favorite of Theseus.

Book II. Line 10. "The Twins." Signs of the Zodiac. Gemini.

Line 81. "Now high as heaven." Chaucer's line is better : —

> "Now in the crop [top], and now
>   down in the breres [briars]."

Line 83. "For Venus, like her day." Friday, named from Freya, the Venus of the North, wife of Odin. In French, *Vendredi*, Venus' day.

Line 93. "Cadmus is dead." (See note, Book I., 499.) The poet foreshadows the death of Arcite and the curse which hangs on his race.   Compare Book III., 786.

Line 114. "I suffer for the rest, I die for you."   As Chaucer has it,

> "Ye ben the cause, wherfore that I die."

Line 115. "Of such a goddess."   The four lines (115–118) have no counterpart in Chaucer.

Line 131. "Cheated."   Chaucer's word here is a singular one, "bejaped," tricked.

Line 157. "Choose thou the best."   Notice the nice point of chivalric honor in Arcite's treatment of Palamon.

Line 192. "His foe professed, as brother of the war."

> "Everich of hem halpe to armen other,
> As frendly, as he were his owen brother." — *Chaucer*.

Line 218. "For sure."   Lines 218 and 219 are not expressive of Dryden's belief.   The idea is in the original.

Line 227. "Hippolyta."   The Queen of the Amazons, whom Theseus conquered and married.

Line 252. Compare lines 252–254 with Chaucer's words, showing difference in style.

> "And at a stert, he was betwixt hem two,
> And pullèd out a swerd and crièd, ho !
> No more, up peine of lesing of your hed."

Line 350. "The power of Love."   The simplicity and directness of Chaucer are seen in his version, as contrasted with Dryden's (lines 350–353).

> "The god of love ! a ! *benedicite*,
> How mighty and how grete a lord is he !"

Chaucer strangely mixes up Pagan and Christian things, as in the use of *benedicite* by the Pagan Theseus.   He also speaks of Sunday and Monday at Athens.

Line 498. "The Idalian mount."   In Cyprus.   Virgil's "Æneid," I., 680. — "Citheron."   Mountain range between Bœotia and Attica.

Line 502. "Narcissus."   A fabled youth, who saw his own reflection in a pool, and, falling in love with it, gradually wasted away. See the story in Ovid's "Metam." III., 341.

Line 505. "Medea's charms."   Daughter of King of Colchis. Wife of Jason, the Argonaut.   Read art. Jason, in Smith's "Dictionary.'' — ''Circean feasts.''   Circe changed Ulysses' followers into swine. (See ''Odyssey,'' Lib. X.)

Line 558. ''A tun about.'' Of the circumference of a tun.

Line 604. ''There saw I Mars his ides.'' An anachronism, of which Chaucer was conscious, giving it as a prophecy.

> ''All be that thilke time they were unborne,
> Yet was hir deth depeinted therbeforne.''

Line 623. ''Calisto.'' One of Diana's attendant maidens. Being changed by Juno into a bear, she was slain by Diana, and placed by Jove in the constellation of the Great Bear.

Line 627. ''Actæon.'' He discovered Diana bathing, was changed into a stag, and devoured by her dogs.

Line 631. ''Peneian Daphne.'' Daughter of Peneus. She was changed into a laurel. See art. Daphne, Smith's ''Dictionary.''

Line 634. ''Calydonian beast.'' The boar killed by Meleager and Atalanta. See art. Atalanta (*Ibid.*).

Line 635. ''Œnides.'' See art. Œneus, Smith's ''Dictionary.''

Line 636. ''Atalanta.'' (Art. Atalanta.)

Line 639. ''The Volscian queen.'' Camilla, slain in the war between Æneas and Turnus. ''Camilla'' means youthful priestess of Diana.

Line 654. ''Lucina.'' Goddess of light. Surname of Juno and Diana.

Line 661. Lines 661–662 were interpolated by Dryden ; a hint for patronage.

Book III. Line 16. ''On British ground.'' Chaucer's rendering is :

> ''Were it in Englelond, or elleswher,
> They wold, hir thankes, willen to be ther.
> To fight for a lady, a ! *benedicite,*
> It were a lusty sighte for to se.''

Line 28. ''Juppon.'' Doublet, a short, close-fitting coat.

Line 30. ''Lycurgus.'' King of the Edones, in Thrace. See Art. Lycurgus, in Smith's ''Dictionary,'' for his story.

Line 120. ''Phosphor.'' The morning star. Palamon set out for the temple of Venus, before sunrise ; Emily, to the temple of Diana, at sunrise ; Arcite, to the temple of Mars, the fourth hour of the day. Different parts of the day belonged, for worship, to the various deities.

Line 147. ''Adonis.'' See art. Adonis, Smith's ''Dictionary.''

Line 172. "Cut below your line." Let the Fates sever another part of the thread, and not that which belongs to Venus.

Line 187. "He knew his boon was granted." Palamon received a propitious omen. Emily, an oracular response which left her in some doubt. Arcite, who asked only victory, a favorable answer to that request.

Line 369. "Raised a strife above." Venus and Mars had granted what seemed impossible for both to give.

Line 375. "Saturn." One of the oldest mythological deities.

Line 386. "He soothed the Goddess, while he gulled the God." The result will explain this passage. The story-teller's art is shown in the apparent confusion and its final adjustment.

Line 402. Lines 402 and 403 are Dryden's interpolation.

Line 468. "Their wagers back their wishes." Chaucer has nothing of "wagers."

Line 574. Quoted by Walter Scott, in "Ivanhoe," Chap. VIII.

Line 671. "Till Saturn said." Chaucer's lines are more terse, without the coarse expression, "blustering fool" : —

"Saturnus sayde: Daughter hold thy pees [peace].
Mars hath his will, his knight has all his bone [boon].
And by min hed, thou shalt ben esed [eased] sone."

Line 766. "Gained hardly, against right." This must be conceded with limitations.

Line 772. "No language can express." See previous note on this speech of the dying Arcite ; also the remarks in the Introduction.

Line 794. Compare the lines 794–799 with Chaucer's : —

"Farewel my swete, farewel min Emelie,
And softe take me in your armès twey [two],
For love of God, and herkeneth what I sey."

Line 838. "But whither went his soul." Chaucer says : —

"His spirit changed hous, and wente ther,
As I came never, I cannot tellen wher."

Line 841. Lines 841–847 are Dryden's.

Line 848. "In Palamon, a manly grief." Chaucer uses "houleth," which Dryden uses elsewhere, but not in any ignoble sense.

Line 864. "But Hector was not there." An allowable anachronism, as the allusion is by the story-teller, and not by any of the personages in the story.

Line 808. "When thou hast gold enough." This is taken literally from Chaucer, showing the low estimate of the sex in general, in ancient times.

Line 869. "Theseus himself." The king appears to have deeply mourned for Arcite; perhaps because Arcite had been in his own household and a favorite.

Line 886. "And so they would have been, had Theseus died." This is a touch of sarcastic humor, on the part of Dryden.

Line 902. "Disinherited." Chaucer says:—

> "The goddes rannen up and doun,"

without the added pleasantry of Dryden's "howling o'er the plain."

Line 992. "The warlike wakes." Dryden, as well as Chaucer, seems to have confounded the Wake-plays, as they were called, of a later period, with the Funeral-games of the ancients. Compare "Troilus," V. 303.

Line 1017. "The attentive audience." The Athenian subjects might have listened attentively to this long "marriage-oration" of their king; but it seems as if Chaucer, or the original story-teller, felt that some sort of an apology was due from the king to modern readers, for he makes the king say at the end:—

> "What may I conclude of this long serie,
> But after sorwe, I rede us to be merie."

Line 1129. "He said; she blushed; and as o'erawed by might,
>   Seemed to give Theseus what she gave the knight."

From the plea which the king addresses to Emily, a doubt remains in the reader's mind whether the lady accepted her suitor from pity and mercy, or from love. However, since Dryden assures us that

> "All of a tenor was their after-life,"

perhaps we may be as pleased as Venus was to have the hero

> "Obtain the conquest though he lost the fight."

CHOICE LITERATURE VOLUMES.

The Silver Series of English Classics. Edited by Prof. F. L. PATTEE, A. S. TWOMBLY, and others. With Critical and Explanatory Notes. This series furnishes editions of standard classics in English and American literature, in the best possible form for reading and study. Twelve volumes now ready: MACAULAY'S Essay on Milton; WEBSTER'S First Oration on Bunker Hill Monument; DE QUINCEY'S Flight of a Tartar Tribe; COLERIDGE'S The Rime of the Ancient Mariner; ADDISON'S Sir Roger de Coverley Papers; MILTON'S Paradise Lost, Books I. and II.; 18 cents each. BURKE'S Speech on Conciliation with the American Colonies ; MACAULAY'S Essay on Addison; POPE'S Translation of Homer's Iliad, Books I., VI., XXII., XXIV., 24 cents each. SHAKESPEARE'S Macbeth ; TENNYSON'S The Princess; 28 cents each. SOUTHEY'S Life of Nelson, 36 cents. DRYDEN'S Palamon and Arcite, 18 cents; CARLYLE'S Essay on Burns, 28 cents.

A History of American Literature. By FRED LEWIS PATTEE, M.A., Professor of English and Rhetoric, Penn. State College. 12mo, cloth, $1.20.

Reading Courses in American Literature. By F. L. PATTEE, M.A. 12mo, cloth, 36 cents.

American Writers of To-Day. By HENRY C. VEDDER. A critical analysis of nineteen contemporary authors. 12mo, cloth, $1.50.

Topical Notes on American Authors. By LUCY TAPPAN, Teacher of English in the Central High School, Minneapolis, Minn. 12mo, cloth, $1.00.

Foundation Studies in Literature. By MARGARET S. MOONEY, Teacher of Literature and Rhetoric, State Normal College, Albany, N. Y. Popular classic myths and their rendering by famous poets; beautifully illustrated. 12mo, cloth, $1.25.

The Sketch Book. By WASHINGTON IRVING. Edited, with Notes, by James CHALMERS, Ph.D., LL.D., President of State Normal School, Platteville, Wis. 12mo, cloth, 60 cents.

Shakespeare. Edited, with critical comments and suggestions, by HOMER B. SPRAGUE, A.M., Ph.D. Admirably adapted to use in classes, literary clubs, and for private reading. 7 vols. now ready: "Merchant of Venice," "Macbeth," "Hamlet," "Julius Cæsar," "As You Like It," "The Tempest," and "A Midsummer Night's Dream." 12mo, cloth, 48 cents each; paper covers, 30 cents each.

The Vicar of Wakefield. By OLIVER GOLDSMITH. Edited, with Notes, by HOMER B. SPRAGUE, A.M., Ph.D. 12mo, cloth, 48 cents; paper covers, 30 cents.

The Lady of the Lake. By Sir WALTER SCOTT. Edited, with Notes, by HOMER B. SPRAGUE, A.M., Ph.D. 12mo, cloth, 48 cents; paper covers, 30 cents.

Select Minor Poems of John Milton. Edited by JAMES E. THOMAS, B.A. (Harvard), Teacher of English in Boys' English High School, Boston. With Biography, Notes, etc. 12mo, cloth, 48 cents; paper covers, 30 cents.

Studies in German Literature: Lessing. With Representative Selections (translated), including " Nathan the Wise," with Notes. By EURETTA A. HOYLES. 12mo, cloth, 48 cents.

Select English Classics. Selected and edited, with Notes, by JAMES BALDWIN, Ph.D. 4 vols. now ready: "Six Centuries of English Poetry," "The Famous Allegories," "The Book of Elegies," "Choice English Lyrics." 12mo, cloth, 72 cents each.

The Masterpieces of Michelangelo and Milton. By ALEXANDER S. TWOMBLY. With seventeen beautiful illustrations. 8vo, cloth, $1.50.

The Sources of Spenser's Classical Mythology. By ALICE ELIZABETH SAWTELLE, Ph.D. (Yale). 12mo, cloth, 90 cents.

English Masterpiece Course. By A. H. WELSH, A.M. Seven groups of authors with lists of characteristic books. 12mo, cloth, 75 cents.

Essentials of English. By A. H. WELSH, A.M. 12mo, cloth, 90 cents.

Complete Rhetoric. By A. H. WELSH, A.M. 12mo, cloth, $1.12.

Send for our Illustrated Catalogue and for Descriptive Circulars of our Superior Text-Books. Correspondence about any books on our list is respectfully solicited.

SILVER, BURDETT & COMPANY, Publishers.

BOSTON.   NEW YORK.   CHICAGO.   PHILADELPHIA.